A MIDWINTER
NIGHT'S DREAM

A Midwinter Night's Dream

Copyright © 2018 Tiffany Reisz

Cover design and layout by Andrew Shaffer

Front cover image used under license from iStock by Getty Images. Interior title page image used under license from Shutterstock.

Mass-Market Paperback ISBN: 978-1-949769-19-7.

www.8thcirclepress.com

First Edition

TIFFANY REISZ

A Midwinter Night's Dream

8TH CIRCLE PRESS
LOUISVILLE, KY

Dear Sinners,

This year's Christmas story is a little different, and it's all your fault. Last December, I did an Instagram giveaway of two holiday books: *A Christmas Promise* by Mary Balogh (a Regency Christmas romance) and *One Hot December* by *moi* (a contemporary rom-com set in a ski chalet on Mt. Hood in Oregon). I asked readers where they would prefer to spend Christmas—an English country house or a sexy ski chalet on Mt. Hood. Again and again, readers replied they wanted to spend Christmas in an English country house...if Søren and Kingsley were there.

And thus was born this year's Christmas story: an Original Sinners novella set in Victorian England starring not Father Stearns but Baron Stearns and not Eleanor but a reformed pickpocket who is the baron's ward. And Kingsley, of course, plays Baron Stearns's valet...a valet devoted to *all* his master's needs.

So in the spirit of "Once More, With Feeling" (the musical episode of *Buffy the Vampire Slayer*) and "Atomic Shakespeare" (the legendary *Taming of the Shrew* episode of *Moonlighting*), I offer you *A Midwinter Night's Dream,* an Original Sinners Victorian Christmas novella.

Enjoy!

Tiffany Reisz

Lexington, Kentucky
December 2018

P.S. Finally, an Original Sinners wedding. And of course, a wedding night...

To Anthony Trollope, my favorite trollop

1

23rd of December 1871
London

The baron was dead. Long live the baron.

Those had been Kingsley's exact words when his master received the news that his dearly despised father had finally kicked the bucket. The new baron was properly addressed as "Lord Stearns," "my lord," or, after acknowledging the title, as "sir." Yet, Kingsley and the new baron had known each other—intimately and biblically—since the ages of sixteen and seventeen respectively, and therefore when Kingsley addressed the newly minted Baron Stearns, he did so in his usual manner.

"Søren," Kingsley hissed, then gently kicked the new baron in the shin.

The new baron—"Søren" to his intimates, as it was the name his beloved mother, not his detested father, had given him—lowered his copy of the *Times* just enough to peer at Kingsley over the top of it.

"We're back in England," Kingsley said.

Søren glanced out the train window and said, "What do you know? We *are* back in England. This is why I keep you in my employ. To remind me what country I'm in at all times lest I forget."

"Also to beat me and bugger me."

Søren held up his newspaper. "Yes, also that."

"Søren," Kingsley said, kicking the new baron in his other shin.

"As you reminded me," Søren said, "we are in England again. You'll have to at least *pretend* to respect my rank while we're here."

"Yes, my most honored and gracious lord and master."

"Better. Now what do you want?"

"Will we be paying a visit to Lady Claire while we're in town?" Kingsley asked. Town meaning London, of course. "Or returning to Paris immediately?"

"I hadn't thought about it."

"Lying sodding bastard."

Søren lowered his newspaper again and arched his eyebrow at Kingsley.

"I mean, lying sodding bastard, *my lord.*"

Søren carefully folded his paper and set it on the empty seat at his side. They sat across from each other in a first-class train compartment, which would deliver them to London in now—

Kingsley checked his pocket-watch—eight minutes.

"Valets who wish to keep their tongues firmly attached to their bodies will refrain from speaking when it is clear their master wishes them silent," Søren said. "In other words—shut it, Kingsley."

"You're more rude than usual now that you've got the title," Kingsley said. "And that's saying something. You were a high-handed knob to start with."

"You should be nicer to me," Søren said. "My father's just died after a long and difficult illness. I'm in mourning."

They met eyes. Kingsley looked at Søren. Søren looked at Kingsley.

They both burst into laughter. A train conductor walked past, and Søren kicked Kingsley in the shin.

Kingsley fell sideways onto the train seat, cradling his leg.

"You kick much harder than I do," Kingsley said. Søren merely stared out the window until their train pulled into the station.

They both stood, donned their overcoats and hats, and found the nearest empty cab.

"Mr. Fitzsimmons's office, Surrey Street," Kingsley instructed.

London somehow managed to be both frigid and clammy that December 23rd, and soon Kingsley was both shivering and sweating as the cab made slow progress to Mr. Fitzsimmons's office.

Søren, however, looked the picture of perfection, as always. Grey suit, grey waistcoat, tie white as new-fallen snow, shoes impeccably polished, and not a single strand of his golden hair was out of place.

"You're staring, Kingsley," Søren said. "Stop it."

"Trying to picture you with a beard. Look," he pointed out the window at the men of business on the sidewalks. "We'll have to grow enormous mustaches to fit in now."

"We'll just have to be unfashionable."

"Suits me," Kingsley said. "I've yet to meet a girl who ever got wet from a walrus. Unless one splashed her."

"Don't make me laugh," Søren said, glaring. "I'm attempting to look bereaved for our meeting. Is it working?"

"No," Kingsley said. "Try to think about how much your father suffered. Does that help?"

"It makes me want to break out into song. Are there any songs about evil men dying of syphilis? If not," Søren said, "someone should write one."

"Won't be me," Kingsley said. "I can never remember how to spell 'syphilis.' Never know where to put the Y and if there are two Ls or one."

"I'll give you a dictionary for your Christmas gift," Søren said.

"I'd rather you just give me what you gave me last year."

"What was that again?"

"A beating and then you buggered me. That's also what you gave me for my birthday. And your birthday two nights ago. And the Catholic feast days, all two-hundred of them."

"Yes, well," Søren said. "I'm very devout, as you know."

The cab lurched to a stop in front of Mr. Fitzsimmons's impressive offices. Kingsley paid the driver enough to wait for them. This was sure to be a short meeting.

Mr. Fitzsimmons, a man as round as he was tall, greeted them heartily as they entered his private office, bowing and scraping to Søren and calling him "my lord" so many times, Kingsley thought for a moment they were in church.

"My deepest sympathies upon the death of your father, my lord," the rosy-cheeked solicitor said, hand over his heart.

"Shallow sympathies will more than suffice," Søren replied.

Mr. Fitzsimmons blinked. "Yes, of course. Shall we begin then?"

The solicitous solicitor indicated a large leather armchair. Kingsley stood behind Søren, waiting attendant as Mr. Fitzsimmons sat at his desk.

"I won't beat around the bush, Lord Stearns," Mr. Fitzsimmons began once he'd perched his spectacles on his nose, "you know as well as I do that your father was a very wealthy man. Investments he made paid off handsomely. The estate is free of all debts and the yearly income stands at..."

Mr. Fitzsimmons cleared his throat and mentioned a figure so large Kingsley's knees nearly buckled.

Søren only sighed, however. "He was as covetous as he was cruel. Did my father leave anything to my half-sister, Lady Claire."

"She'll inherit forty thousand on her twenty-first birthday."

"Better than nothing," Søren said. "Thank you, Mr. Fitzsimmons. I assume the rest of the estate goes to the Crown?"

"Not quite," Mr. Fitzsimmons said. "You, Lord Stearns, are also a beneficiary."

"Of what?" Søren asked, scoffing. "A one-pound note wrapped around a rock thrown at my face?"

"Your lordship inherits the title, of course, free and clear. As to the remainder of the estate," Mr. Fitzsimmons continued. "The townhouse at Regent's Park, the family seat, Edenfell, and the accounts...all yours, my lord."

"I don't believe that," Søren said. Neither did Kingsley. "My father would rather have left his fortune to a one-eyed tabby cat in Yorkshire than to me."

"He did insert a condition which you must

fulfill in order to inherit. And...unfortunately, in order for your sister to inherit, as well." Mr. Fitzsimmons coughed.

"Go on," Søren said.

"You will have to marry to inherit," Mr. Fitzsimmons said. He coughed again. Then he said something that sounded like, "Today."

Kingsley blinked.

Mr. Fitzsimmons coughed a third time.

"Today?" Søren repeated. "I have to marry —*today*?"

"Or tomorrow morning, sir. You must marry within one day of the reading of the will. If you do, you and your sister will inherit. If not, then it's all to the Crown."

"That can't possibly be legally binding," Kingsley said. "Banns have to be read."

"Not if a license is procured—easily done if one has rank and wealth. And I understand Lord Stearns is a Catholic," Mr. Fitzsimmons said with some barely concealed distaste. "You'll simply need an official present at your ceremony to validate it."

"Can't Lord Stearns contest the condition?" Kingsley asked. "His father was mad as a hatter."

"I wouldn't risk it," Mr. Fitzsimmons said. "In the event Lord Stearns does not fulfill the condition, the Crown inherits. The courts routinely side with the testator's final wishes, no matter how eccentric, and they will have a vested interest in ruling against his lordship. Your father was..."

"Evil," Søren said.

Mr. Fitzsimmons replied, "I would have said 'cunning.'"

"Yes, that as well." Søren rubbed his temple and Kingsley couldn't stop himself from reaching down and squeezing his shoulder to comfort him.

"Forgive me, Lord Stearns," Mr. Fitzsimmons went on, "but it's now half noon. I don't mean to rush you along, but for your own sake..."

"Of course." Søren rose quickly from the chair to his full and impressive height. Mr. Fitzsimmons rose as well, at once. "Good day, Mr. Fitzsimmons. We'll be in touch, I'm sure. Come along, Kingsley."

Kingsley followed Søren out of Mr. Fitzsimmons's office and onto the street where their cab waited.

"Death by syphilis," Søren said, "was too good for the man."

2

Kingsley waited until Søren was in the cab before giving the driver their address. The cab lurched forward. Once they were moving, Kingsley drew the shades down. They were master and servant no more, but two lovers, alone and talking.

"Just when I thought," Søren said, eyes closed and head back, "that I had plumbed the depths of my father's evil...he does this to Claire."

"Marriage isn't evil," Kingsley said. "Boring, useless, and monotonous, but not evil."

"The last time I spoke to my father," Søren said, "I swore to him I would never capitulate to any of his schemes to make me marry. Now he's found the one way to do it—by using my love for Claire as a weapon against me. I almost want to applaud him for his ingenuity."

Søren's tone was light, but Kingsley sensed the brewing rage underneath his words.

"Your father's in Hell being spit-roasted on the fiery cocks of Satan and Beelzebub as we speak."

"You're trying to cheer me up. It's not working."

"Just get married," Kingsley said.

"Just get married? Wonderful idea. Tell the driver to stop by the Bride Shop. I need to buy a bride. We'll take two. One for me and one for you. Perhaps a third to keep as a spare. Grand idea. Brilliant."

"There's no need for sarcasm. You're a fucking baron with the face of Adonis, the body of Michelangelo's David, and the cock of...I don't know. Some mythological or biblical figure with a very large cock. There are dozens of poor lords in this town who'd sell their daughters to you for ten quid and a new horse."

"You get what you pay for," Søren said.

Kingsley sighed. The time for joking was over. "Søren, you know—"

"Don't." That one word was an order and a threat. Kingsley ignored both.

"Talk to her," Kingsley said. "That's all."

"She's my ward," Søren said. "She's barely out of the schoolroom."

"She's nineteen now, almost twenty. More than old enough to marry."

"She despises me."

"Who doesn't?"

"We haven't spoken in three years. My first

words to her can't be 'Hello, Eleanor. Sorry I left you without saying goodbye, but I was wondering if you'd be kind enough to marry me?'"

"She was destined for prison or the workhouse before you came along and saved her. She owes you."

"I'll tell her that," Søren said. "But I'll make certain you're standing in front of me so that when the gun goes off, the bullet hits you, not me."

"I'll take that risk."

Søren fell silent a moment.

"He knew I wanted her," Søren said softly.

"Your father?"

He nodded. "I took Eleanor in, made her my ward, and somehow he found out. When I saw him last, he mocked me, saying for all my pride, all my self-righteousness, I was no better than he was, taking home a fifteen-year-old girl."

"Your father forced himself on your mother when she was barely seventeen, and he only married when he found out she was carrying you. And that was the least of his crimes. All you did was give a good home to a poor motherless girl whose wastrel father had forced her into a life of crime. You didn't lay a hand on her."

"I wanted to, though," Søren said. "God, I did want to. The thoughts I had..." He closed his eyes, took a long shuddering breath. "At midnight, the night before we left, I found myself standing outside her bedroom door, the doorknob in one hand, a leather strap in the other. She was sixteen by then, and I was twenty-nine. What decent God-fearing man dreams of strapping and sexually violating his sixteen-year-old ward?"

Most of them, Kingsley imagined, but he didn't say that aloud. He knew a rhetorical question when he heard it.

"You didn't do it. That's what matters. I want to slit your throat most mornings when I'm shaving you," Kingsley said. "I don't. The thought isn't what counts, only the deed. You did not do the deed. Not only did you not do the deed, you packed up and left for three years. You are nothing like your father. In fact, you are his opposite."

Kingsley knew what he had to say to convince Søren to talk to Eleanor. He hesitated to say it because it was as manipulative and cruel as it was true and certain. But needs must when one is being buggered from the grave by an evil, insane baron.

"If you don't marry your Eleanor, someday... some other man will."

Søren's eyes flinched, just his eyes, and Kingsley knew then exactly the expression Julius Caesar wore when he saw the knife in his belly put there by his dearest friend, Brutus.

"Tell the driver to take us to Regent's Park," Søren said.

Regent's Park. The townhouse where Søren's sister lived. And Eleanor, his ward.

Kingsley replied, "Where do you think the driver's been taking us the last ten minutes?"

3

Lady Claire greeted them with an enthusiasm most unladylike. Kingsley stood behind Søren in the elegant entryway of the townhouse. Claire, a pretty brunette with her brother's aristocratic eyes and nose, but not his cold beauty, appeared at the top of the stairs in a fetching gown of lavender. She squealed in delight and practically threw herself down the stairs in her rush to greet them.

"Frater!" She yodeled the word before launching herself off the penultimate step and into her brother's arms.

"Yes, quite lovely to see you as well, Soror," Søren said. *Frater* and *Soror*—tender pet names for each other, Latin for Brother and Sister. Kingsley found it stupid, but that was his jealousy talking. He'd had a sister, Marie-Laure. Not that he'd ever met her. She'd died of scarlet fever the year before he was born.

"Spin me," Claire said as she clung to her

brother, her dainty lavender slippered feet a foot off the floor. "I've been dreaming of this moment for three years, and in my dreams you always spin me."

"Must I?" Søren asked.

"I'll kiss Kingsley if you don't."

Søren spun Claire in two complete rotations before he set her down on her feet again, her hands on his shoulders, his hands on her waist.

"Calm down," Søren said, then pushed down on the tip of Claire's nose.

"Very well." She turned her chin up to allow Søren to press a sedate chaste kiss onto her cheek. "I see you've brought your shadow with you."

"Follows me wherever I go," Søren said.

Claire held out her hand and Kingsley kissed the back of it.

"Have you been taking good care of my brother?" Claire asked him.

"He's not dead yet," Kingsley said.

"Well done." Claire patted his shoulder. "Morning room? I'll ring for tea."

In minutes they were ensconced into Lady Claire's cozy morning room seated on yellow velvet chairs drinking tea from dainty cups.

"How is your Aunt Adeline?" Søren asked, as if this were a simple social visit.

"She's well," Claire said. "Went to buy a gown in mourning black. Said if I won't wear mourning, someone in the house has to."

"You could wear green and white stripes for

all I care," Søren said. "In fact, you should. Let's go to the shops and buy garish clothing for all of us."

"Frater," Claire said. "You're stalling."

"Possibly," Søren admitted.

"Do I want to know what Father..." Claire paused to feign spitting after saying his name, and continued, "...did to us?"

"You don't," Søren said, sitting back in his chair. "But I'll tell you anyway."

Claire listened as Søren recounted the terms of the will. Her mouth opened slightly, she gasped, and her eyes widened hugely. And then... at the end...she laughed.

"That is not an appropriate response," Søren chided.

"I can't help it. You always said you would never marry, even with a gun to your head. And there's no gun to your head. It's just me. Father—" She feigned spitting again, "held *me* to your head. He was a clever arsehole, wasn't he? Before the pox made mincemeat of his brain, I mean."

"Claire!" Søren sounded like an appropriately-scandalized older brother.

"Oh, piffle." She waved her hand. "I've been living with Eleanor for the past four years. She's taught me all the good bad words. Shall I go and fetch Eleanor then? So you can propose to her?"

"When did I say anything about proposing to Eleanor?" Søren demanded.

"Who else would you marry?" Claire asked.

"Goliath," Kingsley said.

"What was that?" Søren asked.

"Yes, what was that?" Claire asked as well.

"Earlier I was trying to think of a mythological or biblical figure with an enormous—"

"Kingsley," Søren said.

"Head," Kingsley said. "Goliath. He was a giant. So he must have a giant head. We were discussing hat sizes of biblical figures."

"Did you really mean 'head' or were you talking about—" Claire lowered her voice, "cocks?"

"For God's sake, Claire." Søren shook his head. "I suppose Eleanor taught you that word as well."

"Twas..." She pointed at Kingsley.

"I am the sole adult," Søren said, "in a world populated entirely by tall and abominably-behaved children."

"He means us," Kingsley said to Claire. "We're abominable."

"Cheers then," Claire said. Kingsley and Claire clinked their teacups together like sailors down the pub.

Søren stood at the front window, one hand on the sill and one on his hip, head down—the very picture of deep contemplation.

"Eleanor's missed you," Claire finally said.

Søren turned around. "Has she?"

"I caught her throwing darts at your portrait last week. She has marvelous aim. I won't tell you where the darts landed, but it was a poor choice to be painted full-length, Frater. Let's hope your portrait self wasn't planning on children."

"She's been a bad influence on you," Søren said.

"Yet, I've never been happier. Funny that." Claire stood and walked to him, took his hand in hers. "Frater, I would rather live on the streets selling matches than see you unhappy. The only reason I'm telling you to marry her is because I know you want to, even if you can't admit it."

"I am her guardian," Søren said. "If another man in my position who was like me in every important respect came to me and asked permission to marry her, I would tell him no, absolutely not."

"Of course you would." Claire poked him in the chest, "because you wish to marry her yourself. And if you tried to stop her from marrying the man she wanted to marry, she'd run away to Gretna Green with him after leaving a dead snake in your bed."

"Live snake," Kingsley said.

"True," Claire said. "I hate to break the news to you, but you are her guardian in the same way I am a lady—in name only."

Søren sighed. Kingsley couldn't imagine how difficult this was for him—his conscience at war with his heart. What a blessing, Kingsley thought, that he didn't have a conscience. Made life much easier.

"If you're happy with her," Claire said, "and I know you will be, then Father loses. The last thing he'd ever want is for you to be happy." She put her hands on her brother's chest and gazed up at him. "He drove my mother into her early grave just as he did yours. I have an equal right to hatred, but I would rather see him forgotten and you happy. And me, as well. She's been a sister to me for four years. If I could have one thing from you for Christmas, it would be to have her for a sister-in-law."

Søren said nothing and the nothing he said said everything. He kissed Claire on the forehead. She smiled, triumphant.

"I'll go and fetch her," Claire said.

"I'll do it," Kingsley said. "She might be armed."

Kingsley left and strode upstairs. When he walked past Søren's official portrait hanging in the hall, he saw the holes in it from the darts. Dozens of holes. A hundred, perhaps.

Eleanor's door was slightly ajar, and Kingsley peeked in before announcing himself. She sat at her writing desk in a pale green gown with an ivory lace collar scratching words onto a sheaf of parchment. She glanced at him. Once.

"Can't even face me himself," she said. "Had to send his lapdog."

Kingsley barked.

She looked at him and arched her eyebrow. He remembered the day she demanded Søren teach her how to do that. Clearly she'd been practicing.

"Writing another of your lurid scandal stories?" he asked, stepping into her elegant white and gold bedroom, a far cry from the cramped and filthy room she'd been sleeping in with six other girls, all pickpockets, when Søren rescued her from her life of crime.

"I'm writing about a wicked rogue with dashing dark hair and a devilish smile. A man designed by God to wear tight trousers."

Kingsley was, in fact, wearing tight trousers. Fitted riding breeches and polished Hessian boots with brass buttons. Might not be fashionable, but he'd yet to meet a lady who'd complained about how he dressed.

"Ah, my biography then."

"A murder mystery, actually. You make quite a handsome corpse, even disemboweled."

"Is my killer a beautiful black-haired girl of nineteen? With green eyes, delicious lips, and a bad temper?"

She sat up straight and tore her paper in half.

"Damn," she said, "you guessed the ending. Back to the drawing board."

Her voice was lower than Kingsley remembered, huskier, more womanly. A voice like running one's hand backwards across velvet.

"Lord Stearns would like to speak with you."

"He can speak to the devil for all I care."

Kingsley strode to her writing desk and stood looking over her.

"When the constable was seconds away from hauling your thieving hide off to gaol, the sainted son of a baron—the very man whose wallet and pocket-watch you stole—intervened. He paid off your debts. He bought your freedom. And if that wasn't enough, he took you into his home and treated you like his own sister. I don't care what you'd rather do, you will go—*now*—and speak to him, or I will carry you."

She rose from her chair and remained there, unmoving.

Kingsley smiled. "I was hoping you'd do that." He swept her up and into his arms. If she was surprised, she didn't show it. He carried her to the bottom of the stairs.

"There." He pointed at the door. "Go."

She started to brush past him, but he caught her by the waist and held her in place.

"I didn't want to leave," he said. "I serve him, in every way, as you know, but you and I were close, in our own way. Being there with you and him and Claire, it was as if I had a family again."

"Then you should hate him, too."

"Kiss me," he said.

"Why should I?"

"To spite him. If you really hated him you would. But we both know you don't—"

She kissed him. Her lips brushed his and he pulled her body flush against him and deepened the kiss with a nip of teeth on her bottom lip. A potent kiss, the sort that went straight from the mouth to the groin.

She broke the kiss and ran her hand through his hair.

"You need a haircut, Kingsley," she said. "You look like a pirate."

4

Eleanor entered the drawing room and shut the door behind her. Søren sat at the piano, playing Beethoven's "Für Elise." He'd removed his jacket and rolled up his cuffs a turn. She came closer, watching him play, watching his long and lovely fingers waltzing across the ivories, watching his noble head as it bowed over the keyboard.

One courageous strand of his perfect golden hair threatened to fall over his forehead. She longed to reach out and brush it back. But she didn't. She wouldn't. The piece ended and the notes rang out and died. He looked at her.

"Hello, Little One," he said and smiled.

"I tried to grow as tall as I could while you were gone," she said, "so you couldn't call me that ever again."

He slowly rose from the piano bench and looked down at her. He held his hand at the top of her head and moved it to rest at his collarbone. He sat again, point made.

"I said I tried. I didn't say I succeeded, Lord Stearns."

"We know each other too well to be formal."

"Once, yes. But now? You're a stranger to me, my lord."

He met her eyes once and then put his fingers at the keys again. "Am I?" he said and began to play.

She recognized the piece at once. "Lo, How a Rose E're Blooming," an old German Catholic Christmas hymn. Her mother's favorite hymn, which Søren knew. She'd told him that during their first Christmas together four years ago, after he'd just brought her into his home. He'd gone to six different churches and chapels until he'd found a hymnal that included the song so he could learn to play it for her.

The piece ended. His fingers stilled.

"Eleanor, I need you."

She almost laughed. "You need me? Where were you when I needed you?"

"You wanted me. You didn't need me."

"I told you I loved you," she said, gazing down at him, fire in her eyes. "Do you know how hard it was for me, sixteen, to say those words to you, almost thirty? You, the son of a baron and me, the common daughter of a common thief. Do you know how hard it was for me to tell you what was in my heart?"

"Very hard?"

"No," she said. "It was the easiest thing I'd ever done or said. Because I trusted you."

He had the decency to look away as if ashamed.

She remembered that moment like yesterday. A winter evening at Edenfell and the air was fragrant with the scent of sleeping trees and falling snow. A week before Christmas. Claire had gone to bed early with a novel. Kingsley was likely off debauching his favorite local widow. Søren sat in the low club chair by the fireplace going over the estate's accounts. With his father in the sanitarium, Søren had taken charge of the estate. It flourished under his tender care and so had she. It had been exactly a year since he'd made her his ward. A year of new dresses and Claire's easy friendship and lessons with tutors and dancing masters and horse-riding instructors. And her favorite part—Mass on Sundays with Søren at the small Catholic chapel two villages away. That night as Søren made little notes in his ledger, she sat at his feet in front of the fire and laid her head on his knee. Between one mark and the next in his ledger, Søren rested his hand lightly on the back of her head. With one gentle knuckle, he'd stroked her neck from her ear to throat and back up again. Had she been a cat, she would have purred. But she was a girl in love, so she turned her head and smiled up at him.

"I'm in love with you," she'd said. "And I know

you're in love with me. If you came to my room tonight, I wouldn't turn you away."

He didn't reply, not in words. Instead he caressed her lips with his thumb, a sensual touch that thrilled her even to recall it three years later. And when he pressed the tip of his thumb into her mouth and touched her tongue, she knew for certain he would come to her bedroom that night.

But he hadn't. He'd left the house by morning, taking Kingsley with him. No note. No explanation except a letter to Claire a week later saying "business" had called him away. That night at his feet in front of the fire had been the last she'd seen of him for three years. Until now.

"You abandoned me," she said.

"You were left with Claire's Aunt Adeline who treated you like her own daughter."

"But you were my guardian."

"And I left so I could better guard you."

"That makes no sense."

"I can't explain further, but I do apologize for the hurt I caused you."

"All's forgiven," she said though it wasn't. "Happy now?"

"You're in the same room with me. Of course I'm happy."

She closed her eyes and took a deep breath.

"What would you do if I stood on your piano and screamed my head off?" she asked.

"Quite frankly, I'm surprised you haven't already," he said.

Quite frankly, so was she.

She took a deep breath and temporarily silenced her desire to scream.

"Now...what do you need of me?"

"I need you to marry me."

He looked at her and she at him. In her nineteen years, no one had ever shocked or surprised her more.

"What?"

"You heard what I said." He began to play again.

Eleanor shut the fall-board, nearly closing it on his fingers. He managed to pull them out just in time.

"Marry you?"

"Sit," he said. "Here."

He pointed at the piano bench. She sat. She was too addled to fight him.

Once seated, he began to speak. He told her quickly of the condition in his father's will, how they couldn't risk contesting it, how fulfilling it meant Claire would have a home always, and she would never have to marry for money or security, how if they failed to fulfill it...they would lose all. This house. Edenfell. The money. They only had until half-noon tomorrow.

"Father had sworn for years he was leaving everything to Claire to punish me. I shouldn't be surprised that he lied even about that. I can't support her and you on my own, or I wouldn't presume to ask this of you."

"This is madness," she said.

"This is revenge. I told him, more than once, I would never be the son he wanted. I wouldn't marry, wouldn't have children, wouldn't use my title...I would reject everything he was and stood for and wanted. I went so far as to nearly join the Jesuit order and take a vow of celibacy."

"You never told me that."

"There are many things I've never told you."

"How many?"

"How many things haven't I told you?"

"Yes. How many secrets are you keeping from me? I want to know the number."

He raised his hands in surrender, but then she saw him ticking off his fingers as if counting.

"Four," he finally said.

"Four. What are they?"

"If I told you they wouldn't be secrets, would they?"

Eleanor growled and stood up. Not to leave but to put some distance between her and Søren. She couldn't think when she sat so close to him. He was far too beautiful. Her fingers itched to touch that spun gold hair of his. His eyes were greyer and wilder than she remembered, like a stormy December sky, and when she breathed in, she could smell the scent of him—like frost on a pine tree in a snow-deep forest.

"I know you despise me now," he said. "I'm not asking for a true marriage. We'll have an arrangement. We'll marry, and you can live at

Edenfell with Claire. Or here if you prefer. You'll have a generous allowance. Kingsley and I will return to the continent, and you'll be free of me."

"Not good enough," she said.

"Name your price."

She turned and faced him. "Everything."

"Everything?"

"You asked my price. My price is everything. I do want a true marriage with you and *everything* that comes with it, including your secrets."

"You can't imagine what you're asking."

"Why? Because I'm a virgin?"

"That's certainly part of it."

"There's this marvelous book called a 'thesaurus.' Have you seen it? It lists synonyms for words. If you look up the word 'virgin' it in, you'll find 'naïve' is *not* listed among its synonyms."

"Of course not," he said. "They're entirely different parts of speech. One's a noun, the other's an adjective. 'Virginal' is the adjective form of 'virgin.' "

"'Virgin' may also be used as an adjective," she said. "Example: *He trampled the virgin snow under his feet.* No one would call it 'virginal snow.' That would be snow that's never been sexually defiled."

"And what would you know about sexual defilement?" Søren demanded.

"It was discussed in a religious pamphlet Aunt Adeline made Claire and I read."

"And what did the pamphleteer have to say about sexual defilement?"

"He was against it."

"And you?"

"I thought it sounded quite nice, myself."

He laughed first, softly and she laughed next, just a little louder.

"Tell me, Søren. Please?"

It seemed he couldn't look at her. He turned his head away as if mesmerized by the low fire in the grate.

"Is it Kingsley?" she asked.

"No," Søren said. "If you didn't know about he and I...then yes. But as you do..."

She did know. Her first summer at Edenfell, she'd seen them share a clandestine kiss. She'd gasped and run off. When Søren caught up with her, she'd been certain he would send her away for good to keep his dangerous secret. Instead, he'd trusted her with the truth—that while he and Kingsley both desired women, they also desired each other. They were lovers and had been since they were very young men. She'd loved him more after that, not merely for trusting her but because she knew when he told her he desired women, he meant that he desired *her*.

"I would never ask you to cast him out of your life," she said. "Only to let me in as well."

He said nothing. His face was expressionless.

She touched his shoulder and at once he put his hand over hers, clutching it. "Was I mad to think you desired me? Or simply stupid? I must have been one or the other for you to spurn me and then to offer me a loveless marriage."

"You are neither mad nor stupid and God, yes, Eleanor, of course I desired you. You knew. Kingsley knew. Even Claire knew. But I made a vow—"

"Damn you and your vows to your father. He's dead."

"I meant my vow to you." He met her eyes.

"To me?"

"The night I took you from the police station, the night I said I would make you my ward, you were frightened. Don't deny it."

She had opened her mouth to deny it, but her denial would have been a lie. He was the son of a wealthy baron, powerful in his own right—anyone who looked at him wanted to bow or curtsy. If he'd wanted to violate her, enslave her, even kill her...he could with no consequences. She knew better to think a handsome face was proof of a good soul. Her father had taught her that.

"That night in the carriage, when I brought you home from the police station to this house...I vowed to you that you would always be safe under my roof. I would never give you any cause to fear me."

"I am not afraid of you," she said.

"And I wish to keep it that way," he said. "A wife should never fear her husband."

"A woman has every right to fear marriage. If I marry you, you will *own* me. Legally I will be your property *forever.* Forever," she repeated. "There is no divorcing for Catholics. I spent three years pining for my guardian. I won't spend the rest of my life pining for my own husband. Either we have a true marriage or none at all."

He said nothing. She had her answer. Eleanor nodded. She turned to leave.

"Yes," Søren said.

Eleanor turned.

Søren stood from the piano bench and walked over to her.

"Yes what?"

"Yes," he said. "We can have a true marriage if you insist. You do give up a great deal to marry me. It's not fair of me to give you so little in return."

"Oh," she said.

"You will marry me then?"

"Yes, of course," she said quickly before she could change her mind. She held out her hand to shake. "Forever."

He took her hand in his.

She expected him to shake her hand. He didn't. He lifted it to his lips and turned it, wrist up. Then he pressed a long hot slow kiss inside her palm.

He whispered, "Everything."

5

That evening they were married at the Royal Bavarian Chapel. Søren knew the Rector, and was able to talk him into performing a wedding mass on very short notice. Eleanor borrowed Claire's best white gown and white fur-trimmed cloak. Søren wore a dark grey suit with a matching waistcoat. Claire acted as maid of honor. Kingsley was Søren's best man. Claire's guardian, her Aunt Adeline, was the sole guest, not including two nuns who watched from the wings.

Mr. Fitzsimmons and a civil official were also in attendance. Of course they were there. This wasn't a marriage for love but to secure an inheritance.

The night was dark and cold. The chapel was lit only by a few white candles on tall iron candle holders. The altar was decorated with country greenery for Christmas.

There was no music when she walked down

the aisle toward Søren and her footsteps echoed. She imagined Søren could even hear her heart beating in the silence.

"*In nómine Patris, et Fílii, et Spiritus Sancti,*" the priest intoned.

Together, Eleanor and Søren replied, "Amen."

And so it began.

Did Lord Marcus Lennox Søren Stearns, Baron Stearns, promise to love her, comfort her, honor and keep her, in sickness and health?

He did.

Did Eleanor Louise Schreiber promise to obey him and serve him, love, honor and keep him, in sickness and health?

She did.

A gold band was slipped onto her finger. A brief kiss was pressed upon her lips.

Then it was done, and Eleanor—the daughter of impoverished German exiles from the failed revolutions of 1848—was now Lady Eleanor, Baroness Stearns.

They returned to the townhouse in Regent's Park. Eleanor ate a late supper with Claire while the men ensconced themselves in the drawing room, drinking port and discussing the transfer of the old baron's properties.

"Nice to know we won't be out on the streets," Claire said after the servants cleared away the dishes. "I doubt I'd survive long. I'm fragile and easily susceptible to cold."

"Like every member of the aristocracy, you're

spoiled and pampered and mostly useless," Eleanor said.

"Are you happy?" Claire squeezed Eleanor's hand.

Eleanor forced a smile. "Never happier."

They left the dining room and Eleanor saw Søren and Kingsley in the hallway, saying their goodbyes to the solicitor, Mr. Fitzsimmons. The man bowed to her and said, "Goodnight, Lady Stearns. My heartiest congratulations."

"Thank you," she replied.

"Lady Stearns," Claire said to herself. "That used to be my mother. Now it's my sister."

"Eleanor, I need a word with you," Søren said.

Eleanor looked at Claire but there was no escape. She was married now.

"Goodnight," Claire said and kissed her on the cheek. Eleanor went into the drawing room with Søren.

"Where's Kingsley?" Eleanor asked. Søren stood by the fireplace, warming himself. She joined him.

"Sending a telegram to the staff at Edenfell. We'll go there tomorrow, if that's acceptable to you. The news of my sudden marriage will be all over town by morning. Claire will stay behind for a few days to put out the worst of the rumors. She'll join us on New Year's."

"That's acceptable, yes."

"I know you always liked it there," he said. Then, "Sleep well. We'll leave early."

She knew she was being dismissed and wouldn't stand for it.

"You promised to give me everything, Søren."

"Yes, but I didn't promise to give you everything *tonight*."

"I'll go to bed," she said. "But I'll say to you now what I said to you three years ago. I love you, and I know you love me. If you come to my room tonight, I won't turn you away."

With that, she went upstairs and into her bedroom.

THIS FUCKING marriage had better work or Kingsley was going to dig the old baron out of his grave just for the pleasure of kicking the corpse. He sat in Søren's bedroom by the fire, drinking brandy when he heard footsteps in the hall, heavy and male. A moment later, a door opened to Søren's bedchamber.

"There you are," Søren said, shutting the door behind him.

"Here I am. Brandy?"

"Immediately," Søren said.

Kingsley grinned and stood slowly, feigning a relaxed languor he did not feel. He poured a steep brandy and passed the snifter to Søren.

Søren drank and deeply while Kingsley watched, merely sipping his brandy. He sensed an interesting conversation was about to take place, but he knew better than to try to get Søren talking before he was ready or willing.

When the brandy snifter was empty, Søren set it on Kingsley's fireplace mantel.

"I have a problem," Søren said.

"Oh?" Kingsley smiled behind his own brandy. "Do you?"

"I want her."

"I knew you were depraved, but you've gone too far this time. You want to bed your own wife? You disgust me."

"You can't be serious for one minute?" Søren demanded.

"Fine. I'll be serious. If you want her, have her."

Søren turned and rested his elbows on the mantel. Kingsley leaned back against it, next to Søren.

"I don't beat women."

"First time for everything," Kingsley said.

"I'm having a moral crisis, and you're making jokes again."

"I confess I am enjoying this a little." Kingsley took his brandy glass off the mantel. "Seeing you flagellating yourself like a medieval monk for the shameful sin of wanting to make love to your own wife. It's entertaining. Better than the opera."

"It's not the sex that is the issue at hand," Søren said. "How many times do I have to tell you—"

"Yes, I know. You don't beat women. Although

you really should. It's great fun when they like it. Half the girls at Magda's were twice the perverts I am."

"She invited me to her bedroom again."

"Has she?"

"What should I do?"

"Fuck her," Kingsley said. "Obviously." Seemed obvious to Kingsley.

Søren turned, glared at him.

"She's a virgin."

"What of it? So was I. Once. I think. I assume so at least. Must have been at some point." Kingsley shook his head. "A dark time in my past. I must have blocked it from my memory."

"Why aren't you talking me out of this?" Søren asked. He stood up straight and crossed his arms across his chest, leaned back against the mantel.

"Do you think I'm that petty? That jealous?"

"Yes."

Kingsley threw up his arm in surrender, turned his back on Søren and filled his snifter again. He turned around.

"You're terrified."

"I am," Søren stared into the fire. "This was a mistake."

Kingsley set his brandy aside and went to stand in front of Søren.

"Tonight in the chapel, when Eleanor walked down the aisle toward you, I have never seen you look at any woman the way you looked at her.

And the only time I've ever seen you look at *anything* like that..." Kingsley smiled.

"When?"

"One night when we were about eighteen or nineteen," he began, "we spent the night in the Cathédrale Notre-Dame de Paris. The night, the moon was full. You remember? And it shone through the famous Rose windows and turned the cathedral colors I never dreamed existed. You said to me that night, 'How can you not believe in a loving God when you see that?' You looked at her like you looked at the moonlight through those windows. You looked at her like you'd just found another reason to believe in God."

Søren smiled, but he didn't deny it. He met Kingsley's eyes.

"I look at you that way, too."

"Did you?"

"Yes, but only when you aren't looking."

Kingsley stepped even closer. Søren put his arm around Kingsley's waist. They kissed, quickly but tenderly, and when the kiss ended, Kingsley pressed his forehead to Søren's.

"You are not your father. He beat his wives though they begged him to stop. You wouldn't even take me to bed me until I'd begged you on my hands and knees to do it. I think you enjoyed making me wait and beg for it as you did actually doing the deed."

"Oh, but I made you regret begging for it, didn't I?" Søren asked.

"I regret nothing I've ever let you do to me. Nothing. *Rien.*"

"And I've never once regretted my nature," Søren said. "Not since I found you. Not until I fell in love with her. How do I tell her? How does a man tell his beautiful young bride, a woman he wants like a man wandering in the desert wants water...how does he tell her he's impotent unless he beats her?"

"You could beat me, you know."

"I plan to. Often."

"No, I mean now," Kingsley said, the idea coming to him at once. "Beat me now and go to her when you're aroused."

"And what then?" Søren demanded.

"Shall I show you pictures? I have my collection."

"I'm fully versed in the mechanics, you ass. I can't simply throw open her door and toss her on the bed."

"You could, actually. She wants you to. Come on, what's stopping you other than stubbornness? She invited you to her bed. Beat me. Go to her."

Søren just shook his head.

"Fine," Kingsley said. "She kissed me today and it was incredible. If you won't be a husband to her, I will." Kingsley started for the door.

Søren grabbed him by the collar and thrust him against the wall. Though no force was necessary, Søren forced Kingsley's mouth open and pushed his tongue inside it. Being with Søren required Kingsley to fight his instincts. He wanted to embrace Søren, tear at his clothes, kiss back twice as hard. But Søren wanted submission of the most abject kind. So Kingsley must stand there, back pressed against the mantel as Søren bit his lips and his neck. He had to stand there while Søren opened Kingsley's shirt and pushed it off his shoulders and onto the floor.

Without a warning, Søren turned Kingsley toward the fireplace.

"Stay," Søren said. Kingsley stood and waited, head down on the mantel while Søren retrieved whatever implement of torture he wanted that night. He didn't have to wait long.

Søren struck Kingsley. The pain was swift and furious, and Kingsley had to bite into his own arm to silence a scream. He knew at once the source of the pain. A Scottish school tawse. The pain it caused was unique. Nothing else felt quite like it. Kingsley loved it and hated it in equal measure. Søren brought it down again. And again. Faster. Harder. Quicker. Crueler. Kingsley's back burned like Søren had dowsed it in linseed oil and thrown a match on it.

And then it was over. Søren turned Kingsley to face him. Kingsley stood there, panting like a dog, ready to fall to his knees and serve. He looked up at Søren and found his master's eyes glowing like candlewicks. Kingsley dared to touch him and found Søren brutally hard. Even through his trousers, Kingsley felt Søren throbbing against his hand.

"There's Goliath," Kingsley said, grinning.

Søren kissed him again, as Kingsley stroked him. When the kiss broke, Kingsley forced himself to smile.

"Go and fuck your new bride," he said to Søren. "Do it well and tell me all about it tomorrow."

Søren held Kingsley's neck in his large, strong hands.

"I love you," Søren said.

Then he left and Kingsley was alone with his thoughts again. They were the same thoughts as before.

This better fucking work.

6

Annette, Claire's lady's maid, came to Eleanor's room and helped her out of her dress and corset and into her nightgown. While Eleanor sat at her dressing table to take the pins from her hair, Annette pulled the covers down the bed and built up the fire. Soon the fire was blazing bright and roaring.

"Are you trying to warm the whole house?" Eleanor teased.

Annette laughed softly. "Your wedding night, Lady Stearns. No man likes it to be cold when he takes his clothes off. Anything else, Ma'am?"

Eleanor caught herself blushing. She didn't do that very often...or ever.

"No," she said. "Nothing else."

"Goodnight then, my lady." Annette gave her a curtsy and a saucy little smile before leaving the bedroom.

God, it was humiliating. And what was more humiliating—everyone knowing it was her wedding night and acting like her world was about to be turned upside-down by an act that men and women had been doing since the foundation of the world...or that she'd sleep alone, rejected by her new husband on their wedding night?

Eleanor ran the brush through her hair one last time. She rose and lit a candle in the fire and carried it to bed. As she was setting it in its brass holder onto the bedside table, Søren opened the door.

She stared, shocked, as he closed the door behind him. Then he locked it.

"Søren." It was all she said, all she had time to say.

He strode to her and took her by the waist, pulling her to him. He kissed her.

She was so stunned by the kiss she didn't do anything at first except allow it. She didn't flinch or gasp, didn't move away, didn't push him back. She stood and let it happen. But only for a moment.

Then she kissed him back. She lifted her hands to his chest and clung to the soft linen of his shirt as she pressed her lips to his. His tongue touched her lips, and she opened her mouth to him, giving herself up to him and the kiss.

She felt the kiss everywhere, all over her body. She burned and shivered, the kiss hot as a summer sun, the scent of him like morning frost on a windowpane. He tightened his hold on her, molding her to him. She felt the hardness of him pressing against her lower stomach and it excited her so much she couldn't help but push her hips against him and it. She wanted to touch it, touch him, all of him, for hours, all night until morning. Eleanor tried to break the kiss to tell him that, to ask him to undress, to lay in bed with her so she could explore his body and let him explore her. But when she tried to pull away, he dug his fingers into her hair, gripping her by the nape of the neck, and deepened the kiss.

He raised his other hand to her neck and yanked hard enough on her gown to tear a button as he pulled it down her shoulder, baring her right breast. Eleanor shivered as his large hand cupped her breast, his skin warm, almost hot. Her nipple hardened against his palm, and he pinched it so hard she gasped. At her gasp he shuddered and released a soft sound of pleasure from the back of his throat. He broke the kiss, finally, but only to lower his head and take her nipple into his mouth. His arms were around her, forcing her to arch her back. She dug her fingers into his golden hair and breathed his name. His mouth was hot on her and hungry, and he suckled her hard enough it hurt but it hurt in such a way that she wanted to hurt that way forever.

Eleanor thought she might faint if he didn't stop but he didn't stop and she didn't faint. But her breathing was fast and heavy. She felt she was drowning in sensation, it was all happening so quickly. She wanted to tell Søren to slow down, let her catch her breath, but she didn't have the breath to say it. And he did not slow down.

He rose up and captured her mouth, forcing his tongue inside for another brutal kiss. She'd lived under his roof—ate every meal with him, spent every evening with him, walked and talked every day with him—that perfect year before he'd left her. Never once had she seen him speak too sharply to a servant, lose his temper with his sister, drink too much or lose control of himself in any way. He'd always been temperate, restrained, and in total command of himself.

Until now.

Without a word—of tenderness or affection, of lust or warning—he lifted her off her feet and put her on her back onto the edge of it bed. He pushed her gown up to her waist and instinctively she tried to push it down again.

"Don't deny me," he said and it wasn't a request but an order. She obeyed it because she didn't want to deny him, not now or ever.

His hands were under her gown at her hips and he pulled her to the very edge of the bed. He pressed her legs open and roughly drew them around his waist. He cupped her between her legs, and his fingers rubbed along the seam of her body, pushing and opening her until he found what he was looking for. Eleanor cried out as he worked a finger inside her. Although at night, alone in bed, she had touched herself there a thousand times, it hadn't prepared her at all for what it felt like when it was his finger inside that tight and aching place.

He turned his hand and pushed his thumb in, and Eleanor whimpered in pain. The sound seemed to do something to Søren. His head fell back and his eyelashes fluttered. She'd never seen him like this before. Before she had thought she'd wanted him, and knew what it meant to want him, but not until then did she feel an almost animal need to take him into her body as deep as he could go.

Søren seemed to share the need. He took his hand from her and he opened his trousers. Though she'd wondered about it, dreamed about it, she'd never seen his cock until then. It was larger than she'd expected, long and thick and she ached at the sight of it. She'd heard of women fainting on their wedding nights at the first sight of their husband's organ...Eleanor thought she could, but faint from the wanting of it, not the terror of it.

She wanted to tell him what she thought of it but didn't have the chance. He took it in hand, guided it to the entrance of her body and pushed.

Eleanor flinched as the thick tip of it found resistance. She didn't want to resist it. She wanted all of it, all of him, inside her. But her body had other ideas. Søren held her by the hips, pushed again, and the barrier gave way, and he was inside her.

The agony was acute, overpowering all her other senses. Desire fled. Pleasure fled. Even her love for him was forgotten in that terrible moment when he wrenched her open. It was too much, too hard, too solid, too thick and too deep. It burned. It burned and it scared her.

"Søren, it hurts," she said. Her voice sounded small and young to her own ears. "It hurts."

She clutched at the sheets, and moved her hips, trying to find a way to accommodate so much of him inside of her. When she moved, though, his eyes fluttered again, and he thrust into her, then again. If he'd only stop moving, she could breathe, ease into it, take it, enjoy it, but he seemed like a man lost to the world.

She needed to touch him to bring him back to her, back to himself, but she couldn't reach him. His head had fallen back and his eyes were closed as he worked her on his cock.

Eleanor slipped her hand between her legs and touched herself where he impaled her. She felt her own tender flesh, wet with desire or blood or both. She touched the organ that split her, sliding her fingertips over it as it penetrated her. Søren must have felt her touch. His eyes opened at last, and he looked down at her.

"Søren," she said. Some awareness seemed to come back to him. He touched her face, stroked her cheek. She turned her head and pressed a kiss into the palm of his hand. "Søren," she said again.

He lowered his hand to her left breast, caressing it through her gown. He grew impatient and yanked her gown down again, down to her waist, baring both her breasts to him. The cock inside her slid deeper, touching her womb. She flinched and the inner muscles of her body clenched around him.

"Do anything you want to me," she said, arching her back to show she was giving herself to him, all of her to all of him. "Anything."

"Don't say that, Eleanor," he said. His tone was sharp. She ignored it.

"Why shouldn't I? We're married."

He wrapped his arm around her lower back, lifted her and impaled her.

"Anything..." she said. He withdrew from her and impaled her again. "Anything...anything you want..."

He turned his head and she saw him looking at something. What was it? There was nothing on her night table but a book and the candle still burning.

"Anything." She said it because she meant it. Because she would do anything, allow anything, give him anything as long as he was inside her, spearing her.

Søren wrenched himself away from her, out of her body. He stood at the foot of the bed and straightened his clothes.

"Go to sleep, Eleanor," he said.

"You're going? Now?" She pulled her gown up

to cover her breasts. "Why?" Her voice broke on the question.

"Goodnight," he said and then he was gone.

KINGSLEY WAS HALFWAY through a bottle of red when he heard Søren's footsteps in the hall.

"Coward," Kingsley muttered, thinking Søren had gone to Eleanor but changed his mind and come back to bed. But the footsteps passed the door and kept walking, fast. Curious, Kingsley went to the door and looked out in the hallway. Søren was at the steps and descending.

Kingsley ran to the banister at the top of the stairs. Sure enough, in the entryway, Søren threw on his coat and walked out the front door.

At night. In winter. Four hours after getting married and not fifteen minutes after going up to Eleanor's room.

Eleanor...

He crept up the stairs and stood at her door. She sat at the edge of her bed, eyes wide open as if in shock, her torn nightgown clutched in her hand at her throat.

Fuck.

Kingsley withdrew to the hallway, leaned back against the wall and put his hand to his forehead. What had he done? From inside the room, he heard Eleanor softly weeping.

Without knocking he went into her room. She

looked up at him as he came to her and offered her his wine glass. With a visibly trembling hand she took it from him and drank deeply.

"He left," she said and her voice was hollow. "He came to me. We..."

"Did he hurt you?" Of course he had. There was blood on the bed.

"Some," she said, shaking her head. "But that was...it was...I didn't want him to stop. But he did. And then he left. He just...he left me."

"Shh..." Kingsley said, not wanting her to get overwrought. "Drink your wine."

She drank again, and he stroked her hair.

"Did I do something wrong?"

"It isn't you," Kingsley said gently as he took the empty wine glass from her. "I'll talk to him. I'll make it right. Try to sleep."

She looked up at him, her eyes wide and green and angry. "You know all his secrets. Why did he leave me?"

Kingsley shrugged. "He doesn't want to hurt you."

"Then why," she said, "does he keep doing it?"

7

Christmas Eve, 1871

A t five the next morning, Kingsley was awoken by a light slap on the cheek followed by an order to get dressed. They were taking an early train. Eleanor and Annette would be coming on the later train apparently.

Though he despised early mornings, Kingsley got up, got dressed, and flagged down a cab to take them to the station. They had a first-class compartment to themselves, which Kingsley took advantage of by stretching out as best as he could on the rear-facing seat, arm thrown over his eyes.

"You're sleeping?" Søren asked, his tone scoffing.

"With your permission, my lord. And even if I don't have your permission."

"You don't."

"Fuck your mortal soul," Kingsley said.

"Have I ever told you that you are a bad valet?"

"I'd rather be a bad valet than a bad husband."

"And what, precisely, is that supposed to mean?" Søren demanded, his tone clipped and crisp.

Kingsley peeked out from under his arm and looked at Søren. "You know."

"Do I?"

"You left her? Again? How could you do that to her? And on her wedding night?"

"What did or did not happen on my wedding night is none of your concern," Søren said.

"In *coitus interruptus*," Kingsley said, "you pull your cock out of her cunt before you come. You don't pull it out of the entire fucking *house* before you come. Do I need to draw you a picture?"

"You spoke to Eleanor?"

"Someone had to go to her when she was sobbing her heart out after you ran away."

"I never, in my wildest dreams, imagined that my male lover would side with my wife against me."

"You need to have wilder dreams then, *mon ami*. And don't call me your 'lover.' I hate that word. Implies I love you. I don't. I barely tolerate you. I'm your 'bare tolerator,' if that. Good day."

At that, Kingsley rolled over onto his side, away from Søren.

"Kingsley."

Kingsley held up his hand, fingers clenched, indicating Søren should shut it.

"We will finish this fight," Kingsley replied, "in four hours when I wake up. Until then, I want you to sit there and think about what you've done."

"Have you forgotten who you are addressing?"

"Have you forgotten I'm French? In England you bow and scrape to your aristocracy, but in France we cut your fucking heads off. Pardon me —we cut your fucking heads off, *my lord.*"

To that, Søren had no rebuttal. A sure sign he did feel some remorse. Good.

A little over four hours later, Kingsley woke up. He found coffee and the toilets and enjoyed them both and in that order. Revived, he returned to his compartment and found Søren behind the *Times* again. Kingsley pulled down the shades to give them privacy. If this fight dissolved into fisticuffs, he didn't want any witnesses.

"I am now willing and able to continue our fight," Kingsley announced. Søren did nothing. Kingsley attempted to kick Søren in the shin, but Søren had seen it coming and moved his leg at the last second.

"Bastard," Kingsley said.

Søren lowered his newspaper, folded it, tossed on the seat next to him.

"She said I could do anything to her," Søren said. "She said it more than once, as if she meant it. And for a few seconds, I came dangerously close to taking the candle off the table and pouring scalding wax on her breasts. And if you think me leaving mid-coitus hurt her, imagine the alternative scenario, if you will."

Kingsley's eyes widened. He blew hard through his lips. "Fair point," Kingsley said. "That would throw even me off my game if you hadn't warned me first."

"I'll accept your apology the moment you offer it."

"You'll accept my foot in your arse," Kingsley said. "Just because I agree it was better for you to leave than douse her in candle wax without warning doesn't mean you win this fight."

"What was I supposed to do?"

"Tell her. Just...tell her. Tell her what you are, what you do, what you want. Tell your wife who her husband is."

"And watch the girl who loves me come to hate me?"

"She'll hate you anyway if you keep leaving her like that. And who knows? She might not hate you. She might like it. If she told you to do anything to her...she might have meant it, you know?"

Søren shook his head. "What is your game?"

"What?"

"What are you playing at? Trying to talk me into telling Eleanor about my...proclivities? What do you get out of it?"

"A full fucking night's sleep," Kingsley said.

"If you didn't want us to marry, you should have told me."

Kingsley furrowed his brow at Søren in confusion. "I did want you to marry her. Nice enough way to get rich overnight, marry a beautiful girl. If I was against it, I would have stopped it."

"I kept waiting for you to stop it, to try to talk me out of it."

"I didn't," Kingsley said. "If you'll recall, I talked you *into* it."

"Yes, which is highly suspicious the more I think about it."

"What do you think this is about?" Kingsley asked. "Can't I just want you to be happy?"

"No," Søren said. "You know I know you too well for that."

Søren paused and Kingsley lived and died in that short agonizing silence.

"Are you planning on leaving me?" Søren asked. "Is that what this is about?"

Kingsley only stared at him, stunned speechless.

"You sit there and berate me, swear at me, and insult me for not being honest with Eleanor. But you're not being honest with me, are you? I ask you again: are you planning to leave me?"

"Why would you think that?" Kingsley asked, too stunned to muster a defense.

"You encouraged me to marry her, encouraged me to bed her, and you are now encouraging me to tell Eleanor everything about myself. You seemed determined Eleanor and I have the same sort of relationship you and I do. Are you hoping she can be to me what you are so you can leave me with a clear conscience? If so, tell me and tell me now. I don't know if I could bear it but I can hardly bear not knowing either."

"I..." Kingsley lifted his empty hands to show he was without words.

"You were seeing a woman in Paris," Søren reminded him. "Usually you boast about your other lovers, but you rarely spoke of her. Is it her? For God's sake, Kingsley, tell me."

Their compartment was silent but for the steady chugging of the train on the iron tracks.

"I'm almost flattered," Kingsley finally said. "No, I am *certainly* flattered that you think I could leave you. Even if I wanted to, I couldn't. My love for you is a beast so unholy strong not even Hercules could slay it. Now that I've said that, I imagine Hercules was a mythological figure who also must have had an enormous cock."

"Kingsley."

"No. No. No. Never. I would never leave you. No, a thousand times, no. A million times. A billion. You own me, you know that. You should no more worry about me leaving you than your own hat growing legs and running away."

Søren exhaled and visibly relaxed. "You are being honest with me?"

"Yes," Kingsley said. "I swear on my mother's grave. The woman in Paris...I do care for her. She's only twenty-eight and her husband's an old man, too old to give her children. She asked me if I would...and I was considering it when we received the news your father died."

"She asked you to give her a child."

Kingsley nodded, knot in his throat.

"But if you're married," Kingsley pushed his words past the knot, "and you're happily married then someday you'll have children. And I could be like a second father to them. You would let me be close to your children, wouldn't you?"

Søren only stared at Kingsley a too-long moment. Kingsley waited and Søren finally spoke a command. "Come here."

Kingsley came and sat at Søren's side. Søren took Kingsley's face in his two hands, forcing Kingsley to look at him.

"Yes," Søren said, his tone emphatic. "Yes, I would let you be close to my children. I would let you be a second father to them. And while we're at it...yes to everything you ever want from me. Anything you wish for, hope for, dream of...yes to it all."

Kingsley rested his head against Søren's chest. Søren wrapped one arm around Kingsley's back, the other around his head. Kingsley felt Søren pulling his too-long hair off the back of his neck. Søren kissed him on a tender spot, just above his collar. "Yes," Søren whispered then kissed Kingsley's neck again. "Yes." A hundred kisses were punctuated with a hundred yeses.

Yes. Kiss. Yes. Kiss. Yes. Kiss. Yes.

It went on and on until Kingsley couldn't tell the yeses from the kisses. He raised his head, and Søren gave him a long slow deep yes on the lips.

Eventually, the kiss ended. With his thumbs, Søren wiped away the tears on Kingsley's cheeks.

"Why haven't you ever told me you wanted children?" Søren asked. His tone was gentle now, not commanding, only wondering.

"I never wanted you to think you weren't enough for me," Kingsley said. "It was hard enough convincing you to be with me. If you knew there was something more I wished for, something we could never have, you'd send me away, probably saying it was for my own good or something stupid and selfless like that. As stupid and selfless as running away from Eleanor for three years just because you wanted to take her to bed."

"It was the right thing to do," Søren said.

"It was," Kingsley said. "Then. Leaving her last night with no explanation? No."

"No," Søren said with a sigh. "It wasn't."

"But it wasn't right of me, either, sending you to her like that. It was selfish. When I saw her last night weeping...I wanted to break your neck for hurting her. Then I realized you must feel the same. You want to hurt anyone who hurts her."

"I'm supposed to be her guardian. How do I guard her from myself?"

"I never imagined I could love a woman you loved," Kingsley confessed. "I know I'm jealous. I'm not proud of it but I am. And when you brought her home, I thought you'd lost your mind. If a man wants to buy himself a Christmas gift, it's usually a new horse or a silver-tipped walking stick. Not a young girl he wasn't even planning to bed. And that girl? She was scared witless she would do something wrong and you'd send her back where you found her. She came to me in private and begged me to teach her which spoon to use and how to curtsy and how to address an earl and how to speak French like any well-bred young lady must. She's common as dirt and so am I. Neither one of us knew what you were doing with us. I still don't most days."

"You never told me that."

"I'll never forget when the Earl and Countess of Godwick came for tea. They thought Eleanor had gone to finishing school in Switzerland as she spoke French so well and behaved so gracefully. I was as proud of her that day as any father had ever been of his child in the history of the world." Kingsley shook his head and met Søren's eyes. "Just between you and me...you may not even deserve her. You've never in your life had to work as hard as she did that year to fit into your world. You certainly won't deserve her if you don't tell her the truth. I'm begging you to tell her, not for my sake or whatever imaginary children you'll have someday, but for her sake, and because I love her, too."

Søren kissed him again and Kingsley didn't know this time if it was a kiss or a yes. For Eleanor's sake, he hoped it was a yes.

Eight hours on two trains and then one long carriage ride finally brought Eleanor home to Edenfell.

The winter sun had long set by the time the carriage turned into the drive, but the lane glowed like morning. Four years ago, after a carriage had run off the drive, Søren had ordered lampposts to be installed. A dozen on each side of the lane were lit and it seemed as if she were being carried to a magic castle in a fairy story.

Edenfell was a great grey box of a house, an old Georgian manor, square and sturdy and safe. Her happiest days had taken place in this home before Søren had left her. And her loneliest nights after he was gone.

The carriage pulled up and she saw Søren on the grand main steps waiting with Kingsley at his side. He came down the stairs and did the footman's job of putting down the step and opening the door for her, helping her out.

"Welcome home, my lady," Søren said, and pressed a cool kiss on her cheek. Kingsley escorted Annette into the house leaving her all alone with Søren.

On his arm she entered the house and found no one to greet her, but the house itself. The hall glittered with candlelight reflected off the freshly polished brass chandelier. The warmth enveloped her.

"Where is everyone?" she asked.

"I've ordered the official welcome of the lady of the house to wait until tomorrow," Søren explained. "The staff wasn't pleased with me, they're so happy we're married. I imagined you'd be in no mood for a raucous welcome."

She wasn't and found the silence a relief. "You left early today," she said.

"I had preparations to make for your arrival," he said as he steered her into the drawing room. "You see?"

Eleanor's eyes widened. Søren had brought in a Christmas tree—a fine tall spruce with silver baubles and candles on it all aglow. And greenery decorated the hearth and hung from the ceiling.

"I wanted to give you back the Christmas I took from you when I left so abruptly," he said.

He was trying so hard to please her. Did he still not understand?

"May I show you something?" she asked. "Outside?"

"Of course," he said and though he looked

puzzled, he followed her from the decorated drawing room, through the garden door out to the snow-filled veranda. Eleanor pulled the hood of her cloak up as Søren slid on his gloves. She led him down a pathway and to the old wood and stone gazebo.

"Here," she said as she stood at the railing and looked up at the bright and shining new winter moon. "This is where I would go to be with you after you left. Every night that winter."

"Be with me?"

"I couldn't cry in front of Claire, or she would start crying, too. I told her once how you smelled like winter and she laughed at me. She said you smelled like shaving soap and nothing else. But you do. The snow collects in here and the night wind, too. I can't explain but in here is where I would find you. And I would close my eyes and breathe you in again and again until I had filled myself to the brim with you." She turned to him and found snow dusting his golden hair and his grey eyes glowing silver in the moonlight. "Did you know I wanted you that much that I would stand in the winter in the cold and the snow at night just to catch, for a moment or two, the scent of your skin?"

"No," he said.

"I did. Yet I think...I think you forgot me the moment I was out of your sight."

"You think that, do you?"

"Is it not true?"

"I will tell you what is true." He moved to stand closer to her so she could feel the warmth of his body radiating even through his coat and her cloak. "In Paris at mass, a girl with black hair like yours would attend every day. I would sit two pews behind her so I could stare at her hair and pretend she was you. I kept an orchid in my room because its scent reminded me of your soap and I wanted to smell you whenever I lay in bed. The hart tie pin you gave me? I wore it every day until the clasp broke and even after I kept it with me. Even now," he said and pulled from inside his breast pocket the small silver stag pin. He slipped it back into his pocket.

"You gave Claire and me 'pin money.' I never had pin money before. I thought you were supposed to use it to buy pins. So I bought that for you. My hart. My heart." She put her hand over her own heart.

"Your heart. I carry it against my own."

Before she could speak, he took her face in his gloved hands and kissed her roughly and deeply. This was no tender kiss, not loving either, but possessive and aching and desperate. She had no choice but to open her mouth to the kiss and receive it. His mouth pressed hers open, his tongue touched hers and she moaned. Without thinking, she found herself twining her arms around his neck and pushing her breasts against his chest. He gently but insistently pressed her back against the gazebo railing. Her fingers found the nape of his neck and clung to it.

"You make me ache inside," she whispered into his ear.

"You can't say something like that to me," he said, "and not prove it."

Before she could demand what he meant, he kissed her again and pulled her hard against him. He opened his heavy coat and wrapped her inside it and it was like stepping into a warm room.

And once she was warm against him, he began to lift her skirts.

"Søren," she gasped against his lips but he pressed his tongue into her mouth to silence her. He brought her skirt and petticoats all the way to her hips. In the shelter of his coat she barely felt the cold. What she did feel was his hand, still encased in his supple calfskin glove, sliding along her upper thigh and then between her legs. He wouldn't, would he? Here? And with his gloves on?

He would. He did. He pushed his finger through her folds once and then twice, a third time while she moaned against his mouth. When he found her entrance, the tender hole, he stroked it and Eleanor gasped and thought she might faint.

"You do not hold the patent on frustrated desire, Little One. Even if you did invent it, I perfected it in the three years we've been apart. The three longest years of my life," he said and slid his finger up and into her. Eleanor shuddered as he entered her, and she pushed her hips into the palm of his hand.

"Again," he ordered and she pushed into his hand again. Pleasure rippled through her stomach and hips. Then again. She couldn't stop herself even if she wanted to.

"I can feel your heat even through my glove," he said into her ear. She was too lost to speak. She had to grip the railing behind her to stay standing as he worked her on his hand. When he started to push a second finger inside her, she had to raise her leg and place her foot on the stone bench to open herself to him. "God," he breathed as he went deeper into her.

He gathered her wetness with his fingers and brought it to the knot at the apex of her thighs. He slicked it over her and kneaded it until it throbbed against his finger. Then without warning he entered her again. His gloved fingers felt thick inside her. She could feel the seams of the leather stitching grazing all her tender places. Inside her passage, he spread his fingers apart, opening her and her inner muscles contracted in protest and pleasure.

"I imagined this," he said and his breath turned to steam. "Touching you inside until you came apart in my arms. I had to leave a piano recital once because they played Beethoven's 'Moonlight Sonata,' and I couldn't stop picturing your thighs straddling me at the piano bench."

"You always played it for me," she said.

"Which is why I can't hear it without thinking of you." He thrust into her with his fingers, again, and then again. He thrust with his hand as he had last night when he took her. Though she knew this time he would not stop until she had reached her peak. She breathed hard as he stroked her so intimately, not at all gently but firmly, vigorously, obscenely. "Release for me, Eleanor."

Even if she wanted to disobey him, his searching stroking fingers would not let her. He moved in and out of her wetness, sliding across that throbbing knot again with his gloves as he entered her. Her hips pushed into his touch and soon the most intimate and delicious flutters began. There was no stopping it now and she came, crying out and shuddering. The pleasure went on and on as he stroked and caressed her.

"Tell me again," he said as he held her cupped in the palm of his large strong hand, "that I forgot you."

She reached between their bodies, took him by the wrist and pulled his fingers from her. She pushed her skirts down and smoothed them, stepped back and away, her hands pressed into her lower stomach where the muscles still fluttered.

"Tell me why you left me—three years ago and last night."

"Eleanor, please—"

"I thought once it would be enough if you desired me even half as much as I desired you," she said and all her pleasure turned to sadness. "But it isn't enough. Legally I am your property and cannot deny you your rights as a husband, but I ask you to never touch me again until we can have a true marriage. And it can be no true marriage without the truth."

She pulled her hood up and returned to the house. She was cold now and shivering, and not because it was winter.

9

Eleanor found Annette waiting in her new room—the mistress of Edenfell's chamber. As Annette helped her out of her clothes and into her best blue nightgown and robe, Eleanor examined her new bedroom. Blue and ivory walls, ivory wainscoting, a large brick fireplace and over it, a portrait of Søren's great-grandmother, a handsome woman who had been the first Lady Stearns when her husband was given a barony as a reward for some vital service to the Crown.

The canopy bed was dark blue with oak posts and piled high with soft down pillows and a blue silk coverlet. A camelback love seat covered in striped blue and ivory fabric sat under the curtained windows. All this was hers now. All this beauty. All this wealth. The house. The land that stretched for a thousand acres or more. The trees. The gardens. The stables and the horses.

She would have traded it all for the truth from Søren.

Exhausted from the day's travels and last night's trials, she dismissed Annette and sank into the armchair by the fire with a book she had no intention of reading.

Just then she heard a soft knock on her door. Not the main door but the connecting door between her room and the master's suite. Before she could answer, Søren entered.

He'd removed his grey jacket. He looked quite dashing in his waistcoat and shirtsleeves and his usually perfect hair rakishly disheveled. He stood at the fireplace, arms crossed over his chest, not three steps away from her. She pretended she didn't see him and stared through him into the fire.

"You wish to know the truth," he said. "I will tell it to you though you might not like what you hear."

"Anything is superior to not knowing."

"Very well. But do not say you were not warned." He paused and took a breath. "Are you familiar with a certain tale by a man named John Polidori called *The Vampyre*?"

"Of course," she said. If it was lurid and strange and sensual, she'd not only read it, she'd read it twice. "Why?"

"The reason I left you last night and three years ago is because...I am a vampire, Eleanor. And when I come too close to beautiful young maidens, I'm overwhelmed with an insatiable need to drink their blood. That is why I left you and keep leaving you—to save you from my bloodlust."

She stared at him. His face was utterly serious and solemn. His tone was truthful and his eyes earnest.

"Are you truly?" she breathed.

"No."

Eleanor threw Shakespeare's *Complete Works* at him. Luckily, as it was an expensive and rare volume, he caught it and set it neatly on the mantel.

"How could you?" she asked. "How could you leave and then mock me like that?"

"Because I am a cruel and wicked man. And also because if I prepare you for the absolute worst, then perhaps you'll take the truth a little better."

"I don't wish to hear it anymore."

"Nonetheless, you will. Come into my bedroom."

"I don't enter the bedrooms of vampires or men who pretend to be vampires."

"Generally, a good rule of thumb. But tonight, you will come into my bedroom."

"I shan't and that's the end of it."

"Eleanor, I am your husband, your lord and master, *pater familias* of this family and you are required by the Church and the Crown to obey my every will, whim, and command, no matter how immoral or arbitrary. You are my property, and you will no more tell me no when I give you an order than a chair will refuse to let me sit in it."

"What will you do to me if I go to your bedroom with you?" she demanded. "Throw me on the bed again, use me, and abandon me?"

"I will sit you on my lap and make you look at French pornography with me."

"Oh," she said, blinking. "You will?"

"Yes."

Eleanor rose to her feet and said primly, "You only had to ask."

The master's suite was far larger than the mistress's and as dark and masculine as her bedroom was light, airy, and feminine. While her room held only a dainty little writing desk, his bedroom contained a large desk in an alcove surrounded on three sides by windows that looked down on the lake. The room was brightly-lit— every candle blazing, the fire hot and high, and not one but two oil lamps burning on the large desk.

He sat in the red velvet-covered desk chair and pulled her down onto his lap. She tried to ignore the bed behind them—the grand four-post bed with the silk covers the color of red wine and the fire burning in the brick fireplace.

"Kingsley was kind enough to lend me his collection," Søren said as he opened a large leather folio. It felt delicious to sit on his lap, one arm around her waist holding her against him as he turned the pages of the folio.

"I have a question for you," he began. "The night you invited me to your bedroom, three years ago. What did you want to happen that night?"

The question took Eleanor aback. Of all the things to ask...

"The obvious, I think. That you would take me to bed with you."

"What precisely were you picturing would happen? Was it this?" He turned to a photograph in the folio—a naked woman with voluptuous breasts lay draped over a divan, a swarthy naked man braced over her, his large cock entering her body. Her face was a mask of pleasure—real or feigned for the photographer, Eleanor couldn't say. But her heart raced madly at the sight of it. She'd never seen photographs like this before. Drawings of naked women, or paintings, yes, but photographs? Of people engaged in the sex act?

"I...oh my Lord." She laughed, shocked and delighted.

"Or this?" Søren turned to another photograph. In this one, the woman was on her hands and knees, the man behind her, cock entering from behind. Eleanor could only stare and squirm on Søren's lap.

"Or perhaps this?" Søren turned another page and there was the woman seated on top of the man, his hands on her naked hips and his organ entering her from below. "Well?"

"I suppose," she said. Her toes curled up in her slippers. "Any of them would do. I...I knew how it works, of course."

Her face was burning hot and her stomach was terribly tight and fluttering.

"What did you dream would happen with us?" Søren asked again. "Don't be shy. We're married now, and these are things I need to know, just as there are things you need to know about my desires."

"I stayed up," she said, "reading. I wanted you to see the light on under my door so you would know I was awake. I..." This was so hard to speak about. She was so good at saying outrageous things when she wanted to shock people, but when she was alone with Søren and he was asking her to tell him her private thoughts, she found herself flustered and tongue-tied.

"Go on." He pressed a soft kiss on her neck under her ear.

"I thought you would come into my room and...and you would kiss me again and we would undress and get into bed. And we would touch each other. After that it's all a bit...hazy. As I said, I knew how it worked, in theory. But in practice...I hoped you would tell me what to do once we were in bed, that you would instruct me so I could please you."

He nodded, smiling as if her answer had pleased him.

"I need to show you some etchings now," he said. "You might not like them nearly as much. These are from an illustrated edition of one of the stories of the notorious Marquis de Sade. A violent and depraved man who engaged in sexual acts so brutal he nearly killed several of his lovers. He's French, of course. That should explain everything."

Eleanor tensed as Søren turned a few loose pages until he came to a drawing of a naked girl in some sort of bare stone room or dungeon. Her wrists were bound above her head to an iron ring and a man stood behind her, whipping her with something like a cat o'nine tails.

"This is a flogging," Søren said. He turned the page to an etching of another naked girl, bent over what looked like a church's prie-dieu though it was clear the girl was not praying. A man was using a belt of some kind to beat her buttocks. Her face was contorted in agony.

"God," Eleanor breathed. The room had grown uncomfortably warm.

"You asked me about my secrets," Søren said. "Here is one of them. The night you rested your head on my knee, told me you loved me and invited me to your bedroom...I did come to your room."

"You did?"

"I came as far as the door, as far as putting my

hand on the doorknob." He pointed at the leather strap in the hand of the man in the etching, "In my other hand was that, a leather strap."

"A strap?"

"For beating you," Søren said. She turned her head, met his eyes. He returned her gaze.

"Beating me?"

Søren pulled out the photograph of the couple having intercourse on the divan.

"This," he said, "does not arouse me. Not alone. Not the photograph of it. Not even the act. This, however, does." He put the etching of the man strapping the girl's bottom next to it. "This is what arouses me—inflicting pain. Until I do so, inflict pain, that is, I'm unable to become aroused enough to do this." He pointed at the copulating couple. "I wanted to be with you like this..." He pointed again at the couple mid-coitus. "But to do so I would have had to hurt you in some way, which is why I brought the strap with me. And when I caught myself outside your door, strap in hand, I knew I had to leave, immediately, and put as much distance as possible between us."

"That's why you left? Not because you didn't want me but because you did?"

"A month after you came to live at Edenfell," he said, "you ran away. Do you remember?"

"Of course. I had a cough and I was frightened that I—"

"You thought you had consumption," he said. "It killed your mother and for years after, even a little cough would make you afraid you had it and it would kill you, too," he said. "And that's why you ran away. You wanted to protect all of us—from you. When I caught you, you said you hated me and that's why you were leaving. You wanted to go home to London. All lies."

"I knew you wouldn't let me leave if you thought I was ill. I had to lie." Eleanor shook her head. "Why are we talking about this? It was years ago."

"I had seen my father terrorize his wives—first my mother, then Claire's. He enjoyed making them fear him. He wouldn't always beat them. Sometimes the threat alone and the terror in their eyes was enough to...delight him. Every little cough scared you into thinking you had what your mother had. Imagine how it is for me, seeing his cruelty and fearing, all my life, I am also infected with that same cruelty."

"But I didn't have consumption," she said. "Only a cold. And you are not cruel like your father. Whatever he had, you are not...infected."

"It's simple enough to believe that when I'm with Kingsley. He enjoys receiving pain as much as I enjoy giving it. But no woman in her right mind would enjoy the sort of pain I give him. And if I tried and I hurt you and you hated me for it... I'm not sure I could live with myself."

"I'm confused..." She shook her head. "Last night you were aroused. You did want me and you did...you were inside me."

"Kingsley volunteered to play whipping boy. I beat him with a tawse. When I grew aroused, I went to you. If I hadn't beaten Kingsley, I would not have been able to...perform. Without inflicting pain first...Eleanor, I simply can't."

He took a deep shuddering breath. "Last night, you were a virgin, your body unopened. When I opened you, there was pain and tearing and that aroused me even more. I came very close to losing control of myself. Which I have done in the past and Kingsley's body paid the price for it. You invited me to do anything to you. 'Anything' you said over and over. I saw the candle and nearly poured scalding wax onto your breasts. That's why I left you so abruptly and walked for an hour out in the cold until I was calm again. Because I wanted to hurt you, so much it terrified me."

"Søren—" she began. He held up his hand to silence her.

"There are more secrets I have to tell you. I loved it here at Edenfell mainly because my father hated country life and wanted nothing to do with the place. I spent most of my time at school or here. When things grew unbearable between my father and Claire's mother Annabelle, she would stay here without him." He took a breath. "I was fourteen and Claire was about two years old. I'd spent the day playing with Claire, carrying her around the house, talking to her, petting the horses with her. It charmed my stepmother apparently. That night she came to my bedroom. And...she kissed me."

"Oh, God," she said.

"I was shocked but...she was a beautiful woman, only twenty-four years old, and I let the kiss go on longer than I should have. She invited me to have her, and I did want to, if only to punish my father. Things progressed and I pushed her onto her back. Then I...I held her wrists so hard she cried out. She pushed me off her and slapped me. She said, 'Damn you. I thought you were different, but you're just like your father.'"

Eleanor had no words. Only tears.

"That was when I left home," he said and wiped a tear from her face. "I packed up my things and what money I had, and booked passage to Rome. There I entered a Catholic seminary and began my training to join the priesthood someday. I thought I should never be close to anyone again because of what I was. And I would have been a priest if I hadn't heard some of the other seminarians whispering about a notorious Roman brothel run by a woman named Magdalena. Not a normal brothel, but a place where men went to either beat pretty naked girls with birch rods or to be beaten by pretty naked girls with birch rods. Or boys."

"That's where you met Kingsley?"

He nodded. "After his parents died in a carriage accident, and his father's estate was sold off to pay the debts, he had nothing. He ran away to Rome where he thought he had distant family somewhere. Instead he was picked up by a police officer on Magdalena's payroll. She took him in, put him to work. Very quickly, he rose in the ranks. He was, as you see, quite special."

He turned a page to reveal a faded daguerreotype of a teenaged girl in a sumptuous gown draped over the arm of a fainting couch, her lips slightly parted, her figure a perfect hourglass, an otherworldly beauty surrounding her like an aura.

"You could say Kingsley was the first girl I ever fell in love with," Søren said. "Magda called him her *Principessa*. Princess."

"Oh, she's so beautiful," Eleanor breathed. "No wonder you wanted her." Impossible to think of the "her" in the photograph as a he, even knowing it was Kingsley in a dress. She was simply too female, too lovely...a true Princess.

"I desired women," Søren said, "but I refused to beat them, which meant I could never be with a woman. With Kingsley, I had a beautiful girl who I could beat as viciously as any man. A girl trained to take beatings. A girl who loved them. And after some time, it didn't matter to me if he were dressed as a boy or a girl. After Claire's mother killed herself, I came home to see to it that Claire was safe with relatives—not my father. Once she was safe with her aunt, I swore I'd never set foot in England again. It was only when my father had been deemed 'insane' by his physicians and needed putting away that I finally returned. And it so happened, during a trip to London to meet with Father's solicitors, a girl bumped into me on the street, and the next thing I knew, my wallet and pocket-watch were missing."

The pocket-watch had been a gift from Søren's maternal grandfather, also named Søren. All the pawnshops in London were on alert for it, generous reward promised. That was how she'd gotten caught. There in the police station, while awaiting her fate—hard time in a brutal workhouse, undoubtably—Søren himself came to pay her bail and see about her release.

"Four years ago this month," she said. "Do you remember what I said to you in the police station?"

"You asked me," Søren said, "'*Are you one of them wicked lords who takes poor girls off the streets and does all sorts of nasty things to them?*'"

"And you said 'no.' And I said—"

"You said, '*Pity.*'" Søren smiled. "The absolute cheek. The constable nearly slapped you in the face. Meanwhile...I think that was the moment I began to love you."

And it had been when she'd fallen in love with him, when he'd first come into the police station, sat across from her, and asked her if she was cold. He'd offered her his coat, and she'd been too ashamed of his kindness to accept it, though she had been freezing. He put it round her shoulders anyway.

"Are you angry?" Søren asked. "Hurt? Frightened? Disappointed?"

"I am..." She took a long breath. "Intrigued."

"Intrigued? Better than horrified."

"No, no, certainly not horrified. Relieved, I think, too. That I know what it is now that was coming between us all this time. I wish you'd told me before but now, I do understand."

"I want us to have a happy marriage," Søren said. "If you wish it, we can be as we were last night. I can hurt Kingsley and then come to you. I think with time and patience, we—"

"No," she said.

"No?"

She rose from his lap and went to the fireplace. She took the candle in its brass holder from the mantel, lit it in the fire and returned to Søren.

"Hurt me," she said. "Please?"

"Eleanor..." He rested his forehead on his hand, rubbing the bridge of his nose.

"Did I do something wrong?"

"No." He lifted his head. "Never. It's only..."

"What?"

He closed his eyes. "I have dreamt of this. I have dreamt of you asking me to hurt you. You speak so matter-of-factly as if you don't realize you're bringing every dream I've ever had to life."

"What don't you do what you dream then?" she asked.

"There is no sin in a dream. You kill a man and it isn't murder. You bed a woman and it isn't adultery. But done awake, it is a sin."

Eleanor set the candle on his desk. She went again into his lap.

"But we aren't awake," she said softly. "Didn't you know? All this...you and me, this house, our marriage...it's only a dream. Mine? Yours? Someone else's a thousand miles and a hundred years away. And you know what happens in dreams? Anything. Anything at all. You can swim under the ocean like a fish or fly in the sky like a bird. You can walk on the moon and dance among the stars and touch the sun and not get burned. Or be as wicked with your wife as you would ever want to be."

"Are you sure it's a dream? It feels quite real to me."

"I'll prove it. You say no woman in her right mind would desire the pain you describe, yes?"

"Yes."

"Am I in my right mind?"

"I saw enough of madness at my father's sanitarium to know you are of perfectly sound mind."

"And yet..." She lifted the candle from the holder and dripped the hot wax from it onto the inside of her own wrist. Søren's chest heaved as the wax fell. It hurt but it was worth that pain times a thousand for the burning look in his eyes.

"See?" she said. "I liked it. I want more. Must be a dream."

Eleanor gave him the candle and stood. She took off her robe and sat on his lap again, straddling his thighs, facing him. Then she unbuttoned her nightgown and pulled it open to bare her breasts.

"Only a dream," she said again. He let a drop of wax fall. It landed on the top of her right breast. It stung and burned and she flinched and hissed. Then laughed at her flinching.

"Too much?" he asked.

"Not enough."

His eyebrow arched. His mouth quirked into an almost smile. He let another drop fall. Then another and another. It hurt, yes, but it excited her as well. The anticipation, the sudden thrill of pain, the way Søren looked at her as if he was seeing her again for the first time, and the power in knowing his most intimate secret and playing with him this private game.

She could have taken a cathedral's share of candles on her body to please him but it seemed a dozen drops or more was enough to arouse him. He set the candle on the desk. He lifted the skirt of her gown, opened his trousers, and lifted her up and guided his cock into her. When he pushed her into her this time—unlike last night—there was no resistance. She was still wet and open from his fingers not an hour ago inside of her.

Eleanor moaned, clinging to his shoulders as he lifted and lowered her onto him again. Once fully inside her, he kissed her mouth, her neck, her breasts. She returned his kisses and caresses, finally allowed to touch him as she wanted since her first night under his roof. She unbuttoned his waistcoat, his shirt, touched his broad, strong naked chest, the ivory tower of his neck, and ran her hands through his golden hair.

She throbbed between her legs, throbbed inside the passage he filled, ached where they joined. She reached between their bodies, touching his organ as it split her, touched herself where she ached. Her wetness was all over him.

"Little One," he breathed into her ear. In reply, she tilted her hips and sealed herself to him. And then he stood, lifting her on him and with him, pressing her down onto the desk and there he took her, making her his wife and claiming her as his own. Her body tensed and froze and when she came it was with a cry loud enough the servants would all know that the baron and baroness had a very happy marriage indeed.

Søren buried his head against her neck and held her close as he released into her, filling her with his seed and at last consummating their marriage.

Drowsy and happy, she wrapped her arms around him as he held her again in his lap on the red velvet chair.

"What shall we dream next?" she asked between tender kisses.

Søren replied, "Let's dream about Kingsley."

10

K ingsley sat alone in his bedroom, a book in his lap—unread—and a wine glass in his hand—half drunk. As Søren's valet, he was always close to his master, so when the new baroness came, he heard it quite clearly from his room across the hall.

"Well done, my lord," Kingsley said aloud. "And you, my lady."

Silence followed and he wondered if he pressed his ear Søren's door, could he hear what they were saying to each other. Or, even better, peek through the keyhole...

Someone knocked and Kingsley nearly spilled his wine in surprise.

Before he could say "Come in," Søren opened the door.

Kingsley's eyes widened. Søren was dressed though his shirt was open at the neck and wrinkled and his throat sported a red mark, likely courtesy of the young baroness's teeth.

"You presence is required in our chamber," Søren said.

"Is it? I take it your little talk was a success."

"You know perfectly well it was. Now go into my chamber at once and stop grinning, you degenerate French whore."

Kingsley obeyed the first order, disobeyed the second. He followed Søren into the master suite. The baroness looked beautiful, bright-eyed and well-fucked as she sat propped on her pillows, counterpane pulled to her waist, gown barely buttoned past the top of her ample breasts.

"My lady," Kingsley said.

"Sit," Søren said. "On the bed. We're all friends here."

Kingsley sat next to the young baroness and waited for his next orders. His heart was running wild. Had he once dreamed of being allowed into the intimacy of Søren's marriage bed? Yes. But he'd never expected it and certainly not this soon.

"Eleanor," Søren began, "if you'll recall, during our wedding, as I put the ring on your finger I spoke these vows—'With this ring I thee wed, with my body I thee worship, and with all my worldly goods I thee endow.'"

"I remember it quite well," she said, smiling tiredly.

"I've wedded you and worshiped you with my body," he said. "Now it's time I endow you with all my worldly goods. And so I give you Kingsley, the most valuable of all my worldly goods."

And Kingsley said, "As I am his, I am yours."

"Is that so?" Eleanor said. "I knew when I married I'd receive gifts of fine China and linens. I didn't know I would also receive a handsome Frenchman. Marriage is full of surprises."

To Kingsley, too. He'd never felt so owned by Søren as he did right now. For wasn't this the ultimate proof of ownership? That Kingsley could be shared, lent, and used by others?

"Eleanor is now aware of what I require in bed," Søren said. "Although I'm certain there will be times she wishes for pleasure without taking pain first. And when those moments come, Eleanor? You may have Kingsley serve you."

She lifted her hand and ran her fingers through Kingsley's hair. This time she didn't tell him to get it cut.

"Would you enjoy serving me?" she asked.

"I would," Kingsley said. "Very much."

"Perhaps you should serve the baroness right now," Søren said from where he stood at the end of the bed, watching them.

"Søren," Eleanor said, blushing. "But what if—"

"Don't argue," Kingsley said to her. "Pointless. Entirely pointless with him. Nothing makes him happier than ordering me about. And nothing makes me happier than obeying his orders." That being said..." Kingsley leaned close and put his mouth at her ear. "I'll only obey this order if you wish it."

"No whispering," Søren said. "Against the rules."

Eleanor cupped her hand around Kingsley's ear, ignoring Søren's edict entirely.

"I wish it," Eleanor said to him. "Though I don't know what to wish for."

"Demerit," Søren said and pointed at Eleanor and then at Kingsley. "One for each of you."

Kingsley spoke to Søren sharply in rapid Italian that he knew Eleanor couldn't understand.

"What did he say?" Eleanor asked Søren.

"He said I am an arse, and I should stop frightening you," Søren translated. "Is that true?"

"You aren't frightening me, no," she said. "But you are an arse."

Kingsley's head fell back in delighted laughter.

"You married well, my lord," he said to Søren. Then he looked at Eleanor. "Shall I show you how I could serve you? And then when the time comes and we're alone or you're in need...you'll know what to ask of me?"

"If you please," she said.

Kingsley raised a hand and stroked her face. It was burning bright and hot, like she had a fever. He leaned over her and brushed his lips across hers. Then he kissed her again, deeper. She opened her mouth to his tongue and he was pleased to hear her moaning softly for him.

He smiled down at her. "Like that," he said, "But here." He slid his hand under the counterpane, over her stomach and then between her legs. He felt her warmth and her softness under his hand. It pleased him when she opened her legs a little wider for him.

"Kiss me? There?" she asked, seemingly astonished. "That wasn't in the pamphlet Aunt Adeline gave us."

"I have much better pamphlets," Kingsley said. "Or perhaps I should demonstrate."

Before her nerves got the better of her and she stopped him, Kingsley pulled the counterpane down to her thighs. When he started to push her gown up to her waist, she stiffened and covered Kingsley's hand with hers.

"Don't be shy, Eleanor. Remember...we're only dreaming," Søren said.

"This," she said, "is a very wicked dream."

"It's about to get wickeder," Kingsley said. "Wickeder? More wicked? Fuck, I hate English."

"Less talking, Kingsley," Søren said. "Put your tongue to better use."

"You see what I put up with?" Kingsley said, shaking his head, as he lifted her gown up again. This time she didn't try to stop him. "A brute. An absolute bastard."

In one easy practiced motion, Kingsley moved between her legs and opened her thighs. He looked down at her, at her open body. With his fingers, he explored her—the soft black curls, the red and tender flesh glistening wet, the inner lips so lovely and delicate. And when looking wasn't enough for him, he lowered his head and tasted her.

Eleanor gasped as he flicked his tongue over her open body. Gasped again when he did it once more. He tasted her wetness even more, he tasted Søren's seed inside of her. The cocktail was potent and he couldn't stop himself from wanting to drink every drop out of her.

Kingsley stretched out on the bed, buried his head between her beautiful thighs and served her with everything he had. He served her with his tongue, licking and lapping at her, stroking her with his tongue and lips. He used his fingers to carefully pull back the flesh that surrounded her clitoris and licked the little bud with the very tip of his tongue. Eleanor gasped his name softly and he did it again, and then again, and over and over until she was pumping her hips into his mouth.

He felt the bed shift and he glanced up to see Søren sitting at Eleanor's side. He opened her gown and ran his large hands over his wife's full breasts, stroking her pale red nipples, licking and sucking them. The sight of it excited Kingsley even more. Though he'd dreamed of it, they'd never shared a woman between them before and that it was Søren's young bride, which made it all the sweeter.

He wanted to please his master and mistress more than anything. And to please the master, all he had to do was please the mistress. He worked a finger into Eleanor and when she contracted around it, he pressed in another. He found the soft hollow on the front wall of her vagina—did she know these words or would he have to teach them to her?—and kneaded it. That was the magic touch for her, it seemed. She came then, her hips hovering two inches off the bed as Kingsley licked her roughly. She released a low hoarse whimper and all around his two fingers, she clenched and contracted with delicious womanly flutters.

Kingsley could have lived between her thighs all night but Søren tugged his hair. He rose up and before he could wipe the wetness from his mouth, Søren kissed him. He didn't merely kiss him, he licked Kingsley's lips in one of the more sensual, sexual wicked kisses Kingsley had ever experienced in his life. Søren was tasting Kingsley's mouth, his wife's cunt, and his own seed in one long deep kiss.

Bliss.

"I've died," she said, "and gone to Heaven."

"You've come three times in one night, Eleanor. You aren't dead. You're spent," Søren said.

"You're a liar, you know," she said to Søren. "You *are* one of them wicked lords who takes poor girls off the streets and does all sorts of nasty things to them."

Søren laughed low and soft. "You're welcome."

As the new couple kissed their goodnights, Kingsley slipped out, across the hall, and into his bedroom where he collapsed back against the door and breathed and breathed again.

That had been a rather unexpected turn of events.

Before he even had a chance to catch his breath, someone knocked on his door. He opened it and Søren entered.

"What..." Kingsley said, his voice trailing off before he could ask the question on the tip of his tongue. *What* was *his lord doing here?*

When Søren grasped him by the back of the neck and pulled him in for a kiss, he knew what Søren was doing there.

Søren pushed him against the closed door and began to strip him of his clothes—his waist-coat, his tie, his shirt, his trousers...Kingsley was hard, painfully so, and needed using, especially after tasting Søren inside his young bride.

Then Søren slapped him. Once. With the back of his hand. Right across the cheek. Hard enough to hurt. Not hard enough to leave much of a mark.

"That," Søren said, pointing at Kingsley's face, "is for your insolence." He slapped Kingsley again. "And *that* was for keeping secrets from me." Søren grabbed Kingsley by the throat and kissed the breath out of him. "And that was for making my wife very, *very* happy."

"Forgive me. Forgive me. And..." Kingsley said. "...my pleasure."

Søren pulled Kingsley in front of the fireplace

where a low smoldering blaze still burned. And then there, on the floor, on the rough Persian rug, with Kingsley on his back and Søren over him and inside him, they coupled like two beasts in a forest. Kingsley was spread wide as Søren pushed himself in deeper and deeper with every thrust. The pain was potent and the pleasure obliterating as his lover's cock speared him.

Søren's weight bore down on him, and Kingsley lay pinned by the wrists and split beneath him. It had been some time since Søren had used him so roughly, and Kingsley's body sang with the bliss of it. Søren gripped Kingsley's cock and stroked it, bringing him to the edge of release and holding him there. The organ rammed into him mercilessly. And when Søren released into him, filling him with his thick hot seed, Kingsley couldn't hold back another moment. He came onto his own stomach and chest with a dozen or more powerful spurts. And when it was done, and Kingsley lay limp on his back, and Søren knelt above him and over him that his master said the loveliest words Kingsley had ever heard spoken.

"And that," Søren said, "was for me."

"The baron is dead," Kingsley said. "Long live the baron."

11

E leanor woke from her sleep when she felt the bed shift. Søren slipped in next to her, naked, and took her into his arms.

"What time is it?" She asked, certain only minutes had passed since he'd kissed her goodnight.

"After one," he said. "Christmas."

She laughed sleepily. "Happy Christmas, my lord."

"Happy Christmas, my lady. Now go back to sleep."

She nestled her back against his chest, luxuriating in the heat of his long lean body.

"Four," she said.

"Hmm?" he said.

"You said there were four secrets you were keeping from me. One was that you did come to my room that night I invited you though you didn't come inside. Two, that you must inflict pain to become aroused. Three was your stepmother attempting to seduce you and that's why you left home. What's the fourth secret?"

"You don't want to know, I promise."

"Go on, tell me," she said, rolling over to face him. "If I can take all the others, I can take the last one." She touched his strong chest and felt the steady rhythm of his beautiful heart under her hand.

"If you insist," he said and kissed her lightly on the lips. "The last secret is this...I can't live without you, Eleanor."

"That's the last secret?" She smiled, half-asleep and fading fast. "That's the most beautiful secret of all."

"I can't and I won't," he said. "So please, wake up, Little One. Come back to me."

"What? What do you mean? I'm here, right here."

"No, you aren't," he said.

Eleanor opened her eyes.

12

Christmas Eve, 1998
Manhattan

Eleanor opened her eyes into a room dark and cool and smelling vaguely of bleach. Søren sat in a chair by the head of her bed, his hand brushing her hair from her forehead, and his eyes searching her face. He looked strange to her. He was her husband, of course. Same golden hair. Same marble grey eyes. Same age or thereabouts. But instead of his grey suit and waistcoat he wore a black long-sleeved t-shirt with jeans.

Jeans?

"Søren? What time is it?"

"Oh, thank God," he breathed. He kissed her forehead. "Thank God. Thank God. Thank you, God. *Deo gratias.*"

"Where am I?"

"You're in the hospital, Eleanor."

"Hospital?" Her mind was a fog.

"You had the flu," he said. "You've been un-conscious almost all day. They gave you IV antibi-otics. Do you remember any of this?"

"The flu? No...no, I was with you."

"Yes, the flu, and a very bad case of it. So bad they thought it might be meningitis."

Everything was coming back to her. She'd ig-nored the aches in her body, busy as she was with finals and term papers. Her mother was out of town, spending the holidays with some religious order she'd gotten obsessed with so Eleanor was staying at Kingsley's townhouse over Christmas break. She'd blamed her extreme exhaustion and upset stomach on end-of-semester stress. She'd gone to bed early on the night of the twenty-third in the blue guest room at Kingsley's. That was the last she remembered.

"What happened? Did I faint or something?"

"Kingsley found you burning up with fever this morning and barely conscious. He brought you into the ER. I came as soon as he reached me."

"Is it...Christmas?" She thought she remem-bered Søren telling her it was Christmas.

"Christmas Eve. Nearly midnight."

"You should be—wait—shouldn't you be saying Midnight Mass?"

"Father Ballard is taking my place. He'll tell

the church I was called away to be with someone deathly ill. Not a lie, unfortunately. God, you scared me so much." He moved from his chair to her hospital bed, sat next to her and leaned down and kissed her forehead.

"Kingsley? In a hospital? You sure?"

Søren pointed. Eleanor raised her head and saw Kingsley, all six feet of him, curled up awkwardly in a hospital room armchair, white blanket draped over him, sound asleep.

"He carried you in his arms into the ER. He stayed with you and made sure you were put in a private room. He read to you while you were resting. Even when I arrived, he still wouldn't leave until you woke up."

"Read to me?"

"The book you had in your backpack." Søren picked up the book, still on the side table.

"*Christmas at Thompson Hall*," she said. A book by Anthony Trollope, the other great Victorian writer. "I read it for my Victorian lit seminar this semester. Oh my God."

"Eleanor? What's wrong?"

"I had the craziest dream," she breathed.

"While you were unconscious?"

She nodded. "We were in Victorian England, and you were a baron, and I'd stolen your pocket-watch and you'd made me your ward so I wouldn't go to jail. And we…"

All at once, she began to cry when it hit her

that when she'd woken up, she'd lost her husband.

"Eleanor?" Søren pulled her to him and held her in his arms.

"We got married," she said between her wrenching sobs. "I was your wife, Søren. I was... and you were my husband."

"Please stop crying, Little One. You'll make yourself sicker."

But she couldn't stop. It had been so beautiful and so real and so true. And she'd been so happy there, married to Søren.

Her dream tumbled out in fits and starts. "I was so in love with you, and you were so scared to tell me you had to hurt me to make love to me. But you did and then it was wonderful. And Kingsley was there, being your wicked valet."

"Of course he was."

"Ah, it was so real. It was like being in a movie and reading a book all at the same time. I can still see everything—you and Kingsley on the train. He kicked you in the shins. Not very hard. But then you kicked back, really hard. And Claire's lavender dress and the morning room and you played 'Lo, How a Rose E're Blooming' on piano. And I remember it all."

She told him everything. How Kingsley had been a cross-dressing teenaged prostitute named Princess in Magdalena's Roman brothel. How Søren had left seminary because he'd fallen in love with Kingsley. How he'd had to marry because of his father's will. How Kingsley had wanted them to get married so he could have children in his life. Proof positive it was all a dream—who could imagine Kingsley as a father? Or even wanting to be?

The dream was so real, Eleanor had to remind herself this was New York, not England. She was twenty-one, a senior at NYU, not a nineteen-year-old former pickpocket-turned-baroness. This is what happened when a stressed-out college student took a Victorian lit class *and* a nineteenth-century British history survey in one semester.

"I was your baroness," she said to him. "Lady Eleanor Stearns. We lived at Edenfell. I'll never forget how the house looked as the carriage drove up the lane. All those lampposts, it was so magical. You'd put a Christmas tree in the drawing room for me. There were even real lit candles on it."

"This dream version of me was not wise in the ways of fire hazards." Søren took a tissue from the box on the side table and wiped her face.

"God...I feel like I'm still there." She put her hand on her forehead, closed her eyes. "We sat in this red velvet chair, tufted. We looked at old porn and then we fucked on the desk. And I knew nothing about sex, which should have told me it was a dream. That and all of us having English accents—except King. He was still French. And

horny. You watched while he ate me out then after? You reamed that man. Like, fucked him to
next Christmas and back. Third-degree rug burn
on his back. If he was an apple, you would have
cored him. I mean—"

"Yes, Eleanor, you've painted a sufficiently
vivid picture."

"You also finger-fucked me in a freezing
gazebo, *while wearing leather gloves*, you pervert."

"That wasn't a dream," he said. "That happened two years ago on New Year's Eve. And I
wasn't wearing gloves because I was a pervert. I
was wearing them because it was thirty degrees
out."

"*And* you're a pervert."

He surrendered with a smile. "That may have
been a contributing factor."

She laughed to herself. Her head was splitting
and she was so thirsty and she had to pee or die,
but she couldn't quite let Søren go yet.

"You're here," she said, "but I miss you. The
other you." Her husband.

He gently rubbed her back while rocking her
against his chest. "I love you and always will," he
said. "Here and in your dreams."

When she stopped shaking, he slowly lowered
her back onto her pillow.

"I'm sorry you didn't get to give your
Christmas homily," she said.

"There's always next Christmas."

"What was it about?"

Søren took her hand in his and twined their fingers together, not easy to do as his hands were so much larger than hers.

"Saint Joseph," he said. "He's a mystery to me, always has been. Mary conceived Christ with the Holy Spirit. No Joseph necessary. Yet God still wanted Mary and Joseph to be married. God sent angels to Mary and Joseph when she became pregnant with Christ and angels announced his birth, but when it was time for her to give birth— arguably the most dangerous part—there were no angels anywhere to be seen. She had to go it alone in a stable, never having given birth before, with no one to help her but Joseph. I think that means something, that God could have sent angels to Mary then, but He didn't, because He didn't have to, because—"

"Because her husband was there." Tears sprang into her eyes again.

"Exactly," Søren said. "I suppose the theme was the sacredness of ordinary human love, that although God could have done it all Himself, He still brought Joseph and Mary together as if the love people show each other and the way we care for each other is its own sort of divinity. Better even than angels."

"In sickness and health," Eleanor whispered.

"Eleanor?"

"Just thinking of the wedding vows—in sickness and health. I'm sick as a dog, probably contagious, and you're here anyway. It is like we're married."

"What matters more?" Søren brought her hand to his lips and kissed it. "The ceremony and saying the vows? Or living them when it counts?"

"Marriage is a sacrament, though," she said, smiling weakly at him.

"Love is a sacrament." He squeezed her hand. "Oh, and don't worry. Most priests get flu shots. When you drink after as many people as we do..."

Funny. For Christmas that year, Eleanor had asked for a threesome with Søren and Kingsley. A silly request, as silly as asking for snow in winter in New York. Whether she asked for it or not, she was *definitely* getting it.

She'd wanted to spend the night with both of them in bed. And here she was, in bed, with both of them there—Søren at her side and Kingsley asleep in the hospital armchair. Maybe not as fun as a kinky threesome, but somehow she knew it was a bigger thing she'd received, a better, truer gift.

And there would be plenty of threesomes when she was well again.

"Kingsley," Søren said, whistling softly. "She's up."

Kingsley stirred and opened his eyes.

"Hi, King," Eleanor said from her bed. She waved tiredly at him. "Sorry I ruined your Christmas Eve."

He walked to her hospital bed and leaned over her.

"Not giving me a blow job by the tree is how you ruin my Christmas Eve, Elle," Kingsley said, pointing at her face. "You die, you ruin my *life.*"

Eleanor winced. "Was I that sick?"

"You had a fever of 104. And you were talking out of your head when I brought you in."

"Shit, what did I say?"

"Out of nowhere you looked up at me and said, 'Get a hair cut. You look like a pirate.'"

"I was dreaming," she said.

"About me?"

"You were a former cross-dressing teenaged kinky prostitute named Princess."

"Ah, in my dreams," Kingsley said, hand over his heart.

"Søren also beat you and fucked you half to death."

Kingsley rolled his eyes. "In *his* dreams."

Søren slapped Kingsley in the stomach with the back of his hand.

"Go home, Princess," Søren said. "Get some sleep."

"You don't have to tell me twice," Kingsley said. He held up two fingers. "Second time in two years you've ended up in the ER. Two's the limit."

"Yes, your majesty," she said. Kingsley turned and started to leave. As he was pulling on his coat at the door to her room, Eleanor said, "Hey, King? Thanks for taking care of me."

He bowed his head, magnanimous as a true king. "My pleasure."

"King?" Eleanor said. Kingsley turned back around. "Leave the tree up. There's always New Year's Eve." She winked at him.

"It's a date," he said, then left.

When he was gone, Eleanor used the bathroom and drank a glass of water before sinking gratefully back into the hospital bed. A nurse came, checked her vitals, gave her ibuprofen, and pronounced her on the road to recovery.

"Will you stay the night with me?" she asked after the nurse left.

"All night," he promised.

"You're a very good husband," she said.

"In your dream?"

"I meant now." She squeezed his hand. "Merry Christmas, my lord."

"Merry Christmas, my lady."

He kissed her again on the forehead and she closed her eyes. Then Søren spoke again.

"Eleanor? Did you say...you said in my bedroom at Edenfell in your dream, there was a red velvet tufted desk chair?"

"Right. You sat on it and I sat on you while you forced me—entirely against my will—to look at kinky porn and talk about sex with you."

"There was a red velvet tufted chair in my father's room in New Hampshire growing up. It had been at Edenfell for a hundred years in the master's bedchamber."

Eleanor's eyes opened, opened wide. She stared at him. No way. There was no way she could have known or guessed that...

"Are you serious?" she asked.

"No."

Merry Christmas from Søren, Nora, King, and Tiffany Reisz

ABOUT THE AUTHOR

 Tiffany Reisz is the *USA Today* bestselling author of the Romance Writers of America RITA®-winning Original Sinners series from Harlequin's Mira Books.

Her erotic fantasy *The Red* —the first entry in the Godwicks series, self-published under the banner 8th Circle Press—was named an NPR Best Book of the Year and a Goodreads Best Romance of the Month.

Tiffany lives in Kentucky with her husband, author Andrew Shaffer, and two cats. The cats are not writers.

Subscribe to the Tiffany Reisz email newsletter and receive a free copy of Something Nice, *a standalone ebook novella set in Reisz's Original Sinners universe:*

www.tiffanyreisz.com/mailing-list

Shortly after the harrowing events of *The Mistress*, Kingsley realizes that to protect Juliette and their baby on the way, they need to leave New York and put their pasts behind them for good. Yet he's waited all his life to have Søren back. How will he tell the only man he's ever loved he's leaving him...again?

eBook and Paperback | 8thCirclePress.com

MORE WINTER TALES

Return to *USA Today* bestseller Tiffany Reisz's Original Sinners series with *Winter Tales,* a collec-tion of three fan-favorite Christmas novellas plus a brand-new novella exclusive to this anthology.

eBook, Paperback, Hardcover, and Audio
www.8thCirclePress.com